# Jungle Series

## Written By LI DI

A

A story about
curiosity and secrecy

Valley

Haunted by

Wild Bees

Primus Press USA

**Original Title:** 《野蜂出没的山谷》

**Original book by The Writers Publishing House Co.,Ltd.**

This edition is published by arrangement with Prunus Press USA, through the agency of China National Publications Import and Export (Group) Co., Ltd.

All rights reserved.

# A VALLEY HAUNTED BY WILD BEES

Written by Li Di

Translated by Haiwang Yuan

Designed by Brandy Ding

First edition 2022

ISBN: 978-1-61612-147-1

 Prunus Press USA

# Contents

# Chapter 1

Omaiyo! Omaiyo!

That was the song of an Asian paradise flycatcher, with a fiery-red long tail and a pair of colorful wings. While singing joyously, it flew out of the mist-enshrouded "phoenix-tail bamboo" (Bambusa multiplex f. fern-leaf) forest.It skimmed across the dewdrop-covered roofs of stilt bamboo houses and flapped toward the distant wild banana grove.

Though it was shielded by broad banana leaves now, its melodious song was still rever-berating in the quiet morning air.

Omaiyo! Omaiyo!

The cry startled the slumbering Ema[1] awake in a thatched shack. She asked herself with amazement, "Is it calling me?"

Rubbing her eyes hard, she took a close look. Eep! The morning light had already seeped into the shack through the cracks of the bamboo-fence wall and glittered brightly on the round, silver buttons on her chest.

*It's daybreak. It must be Delong and Weila who reminded me of starting off.*

"Hi, I'm coming! The fairy is coming right away!"

While responding, Ema nimbly put on her short, black pleat skirt laced with red cloth and her coned hat decorated with silver balls. She then rushed to the remaining half of a broken mirror hanging on one of the posts in the shack and looked into it for a second—a routine that a young woman cannot neglect no matter how busy she is.

A gift from Grandpa Enweng to her granddaughter Ema, this broken mirror had been as intact as a full moon the day before. But half of it was knocked off by the spine of a broad machete. It happened when Weila was recounting a tense scene of him and his ada[2] Mowei battling a wild hog during a hunting trip. Weila was so excited that he illustrated his story by holding his machete high and recklessly cutting down as if he were attacking the wild hog. The back of the machete broke the round mirror behind him relentlessly. The

---

[1] Ema is also the name of one of the celestial deities of the Aini people, a branch of the Hani ethnic group endemic to Yunnan Province, China.

[2] Ada is the Aini vernacular for "father" or "dad."

accident interrupted Weila's storytelling, but Ema was still urging him to go on, saying, "What happened next? What happened next?" Meanwhile, in the crescent shard of the mirror, there were Ema's big limpid eyes, in which the pupils sparkled like two black gemstones.

Ema tucked a lock of glossy black hair in front of her forehead into the coned hat. She broke into a smile, and two pimples appeared instantly on her cheeks. Raising her arms, she dashed out of the shack like a fairy flying out.

Outside of the thatched shack, she found neither Delong nor Weila calling her.

Another thatched shack sat nearby, with the appearance of a horse caravan leader, wrapped in a cotton blanket, dozing silently among a thick growth of grass interspersed with wild flowers.

A few golden-colored bees that had just left their hive were flying and buzzing, now high, now low, in the grass.

*Well, these two guys are still asleep. How can they? Don't they remember that we're going to the Wild Bee Valley to collect honey today?* Ema muttered to herself as she picked up the bamboo pipe used to blow fire by the fire pit and went to the shack where Delong and Weila were sleeping. Inserting one end of the bamboo pipe into the crack of the bamboo-fence wall, she put her mouth to the other end. Suddenly, she shouted at Delong and Weila, "You lazy bears sleeping in your den, get up! Even the bees are out of their hives to collect pollens and nectar!"

"He-he-he! He-he-he!" It was Grandpa Enweng who responded to Ema first.

Ema was caught by surprise. She turned around and directed her eyes to the apiary.

She saw Grandpa Enweng crouching by the beehives to check on the bees' activities. He was looking up beaming, the wrinkles around his eyes extending into his greyish sideburns.

"He-he-he! My fairy, you're like a pheasant laughing at a beautiful peacock. Don't you see the dewdrops on the grass blades are already gone?"

*I see! It turns out that like two diligent red deer, Delong and Weila have already gone to the Wild Bee Valley before the red junglefowls drove the evening stars away with their cock-a-doodle-doos.*

"Why didn't they wake me up? Did they fear that they might disturb the birds in the trees?" said Ema pouting her lips, "Grandpa, tell me, please!"

"No, no! The legendary fairy wouldn't protrude her lips as prominent as a pomegranate like you do. Delong told me that you guys had gotten up in the middle of the night to catch frogs, and you were so sleepy that you nodded so low that your head almost bumped against a rock."

*Aghhh, the two guys were making fun of me!*

*When we were catching frogs last night, it was dark, and the road was slippery, and I was tripped by a vine alright, but I swear I never bumped my head on a rock.*

Ema explained silently to herself and could not help recollecting what was happening last night…

Delong and Weila had woken Ema up in a hushed voice. Hand in hand, the three children had walked to the apiary enshrouded in darkness. Somehow, the apiary did not look the same as she had seen during the day, when the blackish rock on the hillside appeared like a lion in a myth crouching by the roadside ready to ask passers-by questions. Who would have known what grotesque questions it was going to ask? Grandpa Enweng once said, if you failed to answer its questions, it would show you know deadly its teeth were. Dimly blue bioluminescent light flickered from time to time in the bushes of varying heights. Although she knew they were the lanterns carried by fireflies hurrying on their way, she still associated them with the glowing eyes of wild animals. According to Grandpa Enweng, the eyes of such wild animals as tigers, leopards, and bears all glowed in the dark. Ema began to feel her legs stiffen with fear. Leading her by her hand, Weila strode thumping and thumping forward while repeating in a deep and gruff voice, "Tagu! Tagu!"[3] Ema mistook it as "Tiger! Tiger!" and became all the more anxious. Only after they reached the apiary and started catching frogs did Ema recollect herself. The frogs were so cunning that, hiding underneath the beehives, they always captured and ate the bees guarding the entrances. A big-bellied frog could consume eighty to nighty bees a night. Just imagine, if they were not caught or driven away, how could the apiary survive? The three children had busied themselves for a good part of the night and caught quite a few frogs.

---

[3] The term "tagu" is an Aini vernacular for "Don't be afraid!"

Groping in the dark, they had traveled a long way to release them in the valley river. As expert killers of pest insects and thus beneficial to cereal crops, frogs ought to be taken good care of.

Thinking of this, Ema muttered to herself: "Well, these two guys! I'll go and run after them!"

Grandpa Enweng rose and said waving his hand, "Don't go after them today, Ema. How can a skylark fly as fast as hawks? Don't go anymore. Mind you, leopards with bloody mouth may sneak out any moment."

"It's broad daylight. There's nothing to be afraid of!"

Leaving behind a trail of laughter to Grandpa Enweng, Ema threw herself into the thickest in the blink of an eye.

With splashing waves, the valley river made two sharp turns near the apiary and tumbled into the thick forest in the Wild Bee Valley and out of the border. The valley river was not wide. As Weila said, he could have crossed it with about a dozen strides if his legs had been a bit longer. The riverbed, however, was more complicated. Where the water was gurgling, it was only knee deep, and even the timidest Ema was bold enough to wade across it. The pebbles covering all over the riverbed appeared to change their shapes with the tumbling water. Silvery lights flickering here and there in the water like the twinkling stars in the summer night sky were silver minnows racing with the current. The childishly cheerful river was singing, frolicking, flowing, and strolling when, all of a sudden, became a taciturn old man, who spoke in a muffled voice. Then, one must be cautious, as the water here became deeper. There might be a huge rock pit at the bottom constantly spewing a kind of dark blue pigments, abruptly dying the shinning bright water black and blue and turning it completely opaque. Sometimes, the river would open an enormous mouth from its surface to swallow all the dead branches and fallen leaves rushed down from the upstream. Many times did Grandpa Enweng mentioned this big mouth in his horror stories about the Wild Bee Valley. He referred to it as the bloody mouth of a river monster. But he also described it as the river monster's claws in two other occasions. Whether it was the monster's mouth or claws, Ema believed what Grandpa Enweng had told her was truth: The part of the river that became suddenly quiet was the most terrifying.

Chasing the boisterous waves, Ema kept running in the thick grass along the river.

In the morning, steaming mist hovered on the river. The oncoming, chilly river breeze was brushing her face when suddenly, splash, splash, a startled mallard fluttered from the water grass. She shuddered and balked, pricking her ears to listen. Gee, the river became quiet. It had become an old man. Without looking at it, she knew for certain that its water was dark green and its mouth wide open. Ema looked back, only to find the apiary hidden in the thickets. She could not even hear bees buzzing. What to do? Ema regretted coming here against Grandpa Enweng's warning. Shall I return? She asked herself while surveying the bushes surrounding her. Crystal-like dewdrops glistened on their luxuriant leaves. In an instant, these dewdrops seemed to turn into countless eyes blinking at her. Among them were a pair of squinted eyes, which belonged to DeLong. He seemed to be saying: "Once shot out, a bamboo arrow has no alternative but to fly ahead!" Another pair of eyes that looked round and a little bulging were fixed on her. They were Weila's, and he seemed to be jeering, "You call yourself a fairy for nothing because you are as timid as a squirrel on a tree!"

Biting her lip, Ema snorted and said, "You say I'm no better than a squirrel? I'm fourteen years old this year, the same age as you are Weila! How can you belittle me? We'll wait and see."

Just then, she heard someone calling her, "Ema! Ema!"

Ema turned around and saw Grandpa Enweng coming after her.

"Ema, the forest is deep and the grass is dense. Many snakes are lurking in them. Don't go after them anymore. You can't catch up anyway. Come with me! Let's go back and fix lunch. When they're back, they'll just be hungry enough to enjoy it. Please listen to your grandpa."

Always obedient to grandpa, Ema followed him back to the apiary to prepare lunch.

Grandpa Enweng lit a fire in the open-air fire pit. Smoke arose from the thick grass.

The mist-like cooking smoke drifted with the wind and mingled with the cooking-smoke-like haze. Together, they looked like a thin fabric of cotton woven by the Aini girls. Caressed and played by the morning breeze, it was rising increasingly higher and thinner and gradually permeated the air above the apiary of the Menglang Mountain Village before dissipating in the thick old-growth forest in the Wild Bee Valley.

The apiary of the Menglang Mountain Village sat on the hillside at the entrance of the Wild Bee Valley. Situated quietly on the leeward and sunny side against the mountain and facing the valley river, it was ideal for bee keeping. Viewed on the hillside, in the remote south were the lush areca palms and the beautiful Menglang Mountain Village in the embrace of windmill palms. Viewed on the hillside, in the north were a stretch of lush subtropical dense wood, which was the Wild Bee Valley connected to the border.

The Wild Bee Valley was an inexhaustible source of honey plants.

The mountain village's apiary was established five or six years ago. All the bee-keeping supplies had been donated by the villagers, including square hives, barrels made of staves bound with hoops, hollowed logs with barks on them, exquisitely pleated bamboo baskets, and big earthen jars pasted with cow dung on the outside. These sundry items scattered here and there on the hillside, contributing to the unique appearance of the apiary. Don't take this farm lightly. As a saying goes, "A candle may burn low, but its light still shines far." Thanks to Grandpa Enweng's diligence and expertise, in just a few years, the farm had increased its bee colonies from the initial eighty to ninety to the current four hundred. The bees not only provided each of the village household with honey and the collective with cash income, but also pollinated the cereal crops. As a result, each corn stalk could bear two to three ears as long as an ox horn while rapeseed developed plump pods clustering on the stem like chili peppers. The two threshing machines newly purchased by the village came from the bees. CPC Party branch secretary Lang Shuai said at the ceremony to receive the machines, "The bees really have strong mouths, in which they carried the big machines to us!" Amid the beating of *mang* gongs and deerskin drums, the villagers sang and danced, vying with one another in toasting Grandpa Enweng with their bamboo tubes of wine. For a time, bamboo tubes clanged with one another, knocking out of them some of the wine. It exuded a sweet and yet intoxicating aroma in the air, which almost inebriated Ema. She clapped for her grandpa jubilantly, her broad smile narrowing her eyes into slits, each resembling a new moon.

Ema loved her grandpa very much. He had told her that her ada and ama had both died of illness when she was young, and she had been living with him ever since. Grandpa had been a bee-keeper all his life and had used to lead a hard life. Party Secretary Lang Shuai and veteran Production Team Leader Ka Bure offered to provide him with some assistants several times, but each time he would shake his head saying, "Everyone is as busy in the fields as a beaver, and you try to spare some labor for me? Do you think I'm old? My limbs are chiseled out of a stone, but not kneaded from a rice dough." So, grandpa categorically declined their offer to help. But, just think of the work of taking care of the four hundred or more colonies of bees. It involved feeding them, harvesting honey, dividing the colonies, and getting rid of pests. Anyway, it kept him extremely busy.

Ema went to school together with Delong and Weila. The school was in an ethnic Dai village far away from the Menglang Mountain Village. So, they had to board at the school, and they would not come back home until vacations.

Their summer vacation had arrived in July. They had rushed back as parrots were let out of their cage flying. They would spend a meaningful vacation on the apiary, learning from Grandpa Enweng the skill of bee keeping and helped him with manual labor. Secretary Lang Shuai took them to see Grandpa Enweng. Running his hand over their heads affectionately, Grandpa Enweng said beaming, "You may be offspring of poor families but now you've got the chance to go to school. It's great for you not to forget your farmer family's original aspiration to earn a living by honest labor. But...." He knitted his eye brows together and continued, "The bees are buzzing around every day. I'm afraid they may drive you crazy. To my mind, you'd better not give up your study. You ought to make good use of your vacation time to do your studies well instead of coming to the apiary to see bees flying and hear them buzzing. That would be a waste of your time and intelligence." Secretary Lang Shuai told Grandpa Enweng with a smile, "Don't worry! The children have allocated their time for their daily studies. Like two flowers growing on one lotus stalk, we should give them a chance to benefit from both study and labor during their summer vacation." Grandpa Enweng nodded his head while listening, but when the secretary finished, he said, "Don't take my nodding as consent!" Then, he surprised everyone by saying, "Nine out of ten beekeepers get stung. This is no easy job. It'd be too bad if you got stung all over. Besides, the valley is full of bears, leopards, vipers..." Before he finished enumerating the terrifying beats of prey while counting on his fingers, the children began to pester him, dragging him by his sleeves and holding him from behind by his waist as they entreated and vowed. Grandpa Enweng finally relented. He said to Secretary Lang Shuai, "A saying goes, 'A tit may be small, but it has all the vital organs; a river snail may be tiny, but it has at least three whorls.' They may be young, but they're all very considerate. I've learned about their secret plan: The Army Day is coming on August 1. They're going to visit the soldiers at the 179th Armory with the best-quality honey they'll harvest." The secretary's remark revealed the children's intention like pealing the sheath to reveal the tender part of a bamboo shoot. The children were so joyous that they hopped and shouted, as lively as the morning birds chirping in the forest. Pulling out the machete from the back of his waist, Grandpa Enweng said, "Let's go and get some bamboo stems to build shacks for you." Then turning to Secretary Lang Shuai, he continued, "This time, we're of the same mind! I've had the same plan to donate all the honey harvested this month to our beloved soldiers in the armory!"

The children moved to the apiary like butterflies getting into a flowerbed. Grandpa Enweng built two small shacks beside his crude, low-lying stilt bamboo house.

Why could they not stay with the kind and beaming grandpa under the same roof?

According to Grandpa Enweng, "A cow sleeps more when it's old, but a man sleeps less when he ages. Not just that I sleep less every night, I also smoke the water pipe, which makes a lot of noises. I don't want to disturb you. You're at a stage of growth when you sleep well and need sufficient sleep."

Obviously, Grandpa Enweng was very considerate.

Now, Delong and Weila had gone to the Wild Bee Valley, and after fixing lunch, Ema and grandpa came to the apiary and set about working: grandpa attending to the bees, and Ema doing the cleaning and tidying chores.

Suddenly, Ema heard grandpa saying to her, "My fairy, I can't see clearly, can you help? Tell me if the bees are swarming for reproductive reasons."

Ema knew that grandpa had no eye problems. He was putting her to a test.

Saying "yes" profusely, she scurried to grandpa like a rabbit.

She caught sight of two hives, one large, and the other small.

Ema directed her eyes on the bigger hive first…

The diligent worker bees were busying themselves. Some were cleansing the empty brood nests, removing fecal droppings and dirt with their mouths; some were cutting open the wax sealing over the filled honey stomachs with their teeth, taking out the sweet content and bringing it to baby bees as their breakfast; some were moving their antennae above the honey comb, preparing for the construction of new structures of hexagonal cells of wax; a few others were crowding toward an invading fire ant to fight and drag it out of the hive. The big-bellied queen bee, clustered around by worker bees, crawled majestically on the honeycomb and stuck its tail into the cleaned brood nests to lay eggs. Populating the honeycomb depends on it. Therefore, the workers were taking great care of it. If it felt too warm, they would cool her off by fanning their wings; if it was thirsty, they would fly out to siphon water and bring back to quench its thirst; if it wanted to climb to another honeycomb, they would work hand in hand to form a ladder. Just then, all the worker bees working outside on honey plants were returning. They were all heroes. Some had their bellies filled with nectar, and some with two golden balls hanging from the pollen press on their hind legs. The balls were the pollens they had collected. The returned workers proudly circled twice around a hive and crawled into it one after another. There, they vied with one another in regurgitating the nectar and scraping off the pollen, to see who had reaped the most. Afterwards, none seemed to accept the result of their competition and buzzed out in throngs. Wow, how energetic the colony of bees was! And that was its norm.

Ema then began to examine the smaller hive…

Oh, no! Things were not going well. The overpopulated bees were packed like sardines. None had the intention to go to the honey plants. The big-bellied queen bee was sleeping languidly in the comb. Some of the bees formed a chain by having others' hind legs in their mouths, and it swayed in the wind outside of the hive, as if it were the goatee of a

Himalayan blue sheep.

Ema cried with alarm, "There grows a goatee! They're swarming!"

Grandpa Enweng broke into a smile, "A young tree will bifurcate when it's growing up; a family will be divided up when the children have matured. The beehive is too small for too many bees. If we don't get log skeps ready, they will build separate colonies. Those leaving the original colony will fly away to find their new home in the Wild Bee Valley."

"Grandpa, can they survive the elements after they settle in the Wild Bee Valley?"

"They have to tough it out like it or not." Grandpa sighed. Then he added, "Once in the old-growth forest, they'll become wild bees. It's like a man who gets stuck in the old-growth forest will become a savage." As he said so, grandpa heaved a deep sigh.

Raising her head, she peered at the Wild Bee Valley, beseeching silently, *Delong and Weila, please get log skeps back as soon as possible so that the bees can have their new, cozy homes.*

Whack! Thwack! Whack! Thwack!

The sound of cutting wood came from the Wild Bee Valley.

A woodpecker who had been boring holes in a tree for worms now stopped to stare at the two youngsters with its wide-open eyes.

A gibbon who had been foraging in the open air looked around, holding a cluster of yellow musa wilsonii. They were trying to identify the source of the whacking sound.

A watering red deer paused, planting its thin legs on the ground. Pricking its ears, it listened carefully to the sound of woodcutting.

Delong and Weila had felled a hollowed big-leaf tree and cut it into four sections. Stopped up on both sides, each became a log skep.

But each of the logs was too thick to be held under the arm and too awkward to be picked up by the hand. How to get them back?

Delong scratched his head as if all good ideas were stored in it.

Wiping sweat off his face, Weila said in a deep and gruff voice, "Well, Delong, don't waste our time figuring out how to get all of them back at the same time. Let's each carry one and leaving the other two here. The dumb bears won't be able to take them anyway."

"I hope we're not as dumb as bears," said Delong still scratching his head. Suddenly, a smile broke on his good-looking, oval face. Blinking his eyes with long lashes, he burst out, "I've got it! We can carry them like a horse pack."

Ha! Delong's ideas were as many as the cells of a honey-comb!

"Like the pack used by a horse caravan leader, we can string two logs together with a vine so we can carry them over our shoulder, one in the front and the other at the back. Then, we can take all of the log skeps back, can't we."

Giving Delong a gentle punch, Weila said, "Then, aren't we becoming horses, then?"

Delong said, "You've got a bigger head, so I'll call you Big-headed Horse!"

Weila said, "You've got a higher nose bridge, so I'll call you Long-nosed Horse!"

Indeed, Delong's nose bridge originally looked longer. His deep-set eye sockets and thick, black brows make it appear even longer.

Delong was fifteen years old this year. The sunshine on the plateau tanned his face; the valley wind of the valley toughened his muscles; and the beast-infested forest lent him courage. People in the Menglang Mountain Village commented that Delong resembled his ada Mu Sade, so much so that they looked as if they were cast in the same mold.

Mu Sade is the commander of a PLA company guarding the 179th Armory. He made Delong proud. Both Weila and Ema also shared his pride. The three children were as inseparable as vines entertained with trees.

"That's great! The apiary suddenly has two horses added to it. How cool!" Pinching Weila's nose, Delong requested, "Come on, perform a mimicry of a horse's neigh."

"You must perform, too!" responded Weila, who reached to hold Delong by his nose.

Holding each other's nose between the fingers, the two boys mimicked a horse's neigh face to face and laughed heartily alternately for a while before they resumed working.

Weila went to look for rattans to string the hollowed logs with while Delong smoothened the outer surface by whittling it.

When taken back to the apiary, it would be soaked in the water that had been used to rinse rice to remove the odor of rotten wood that averted bees. Then, with both ends stopped up, they would become perfect skeps for dividing the bee colonies.

Suddenly, Weila's scream of fear came from the forest, "Yikes, snake!"

Delong looked up, only to see a Tibetan pit viper raising its head and, swaying the front part of its body, charging at Weila.

It turned out that the careless Weila had treated the snake as a rattan and tried to pull it. The "rattan" suddenly moved at the pull. Only then did he realize that it was a pit viper, which quickly launched an attack. Weila swung his machete at the snake with all his might, but the viper unexpectedly tossed its head and upper body aside and dodged it. The machete missed the target. The momentum threw it a few feet away from Weila's hand. Opening its mouth, the pit viper set to bite Weila before he regained his balance.

When the fight caught Delong's attention, it was too late for him to rush to Weila's help. Suddenly, he began to roar in a strange voice, "Owwu! Owwu!" Then he danced in front of the snake, swaying and twisting his body and waving his hands. As he danced, he continued his strange call, "Owwu! Owwu!" No one knows what tactic he was employing.

To their surprise, however, the viper unexpectedly froze and watched Delong "dancing."

Seizing the right moment, Weila grabbed the pit viper by its tail and ran.

The viper felt all the bones in its spine shaken loose in Weila's hand. No matter how it tried to wiggle, it could by no means turn its head up to bite him.

Running a few steps, Weila slung the viper whooshing out of his hand, and it flew into a great distance.

As soon as it landed, the viper slithered away.

Weila said, "Hey, Long-nosed Horse, I didn't expect that you were such a great dancer!"

Delong felt proud, saying, "Ha-ha, my ada taught me this trick. It's known as psychological tactic. Since it had never seen it before, the viper was dumbfounded. But the trick wouldn't last long. Luckily, you were so quick at getting rid of it."

Weila, "Super! Now I've learned another trick from you."

After they cut and gathered enough rattans, they strung the hollowed logs and put the "packs" on the "horsebacks," that is, their shoulders.

Calling each other their newly acquired nicknames while scratching each other's nose, they trudged back mimicking horse's neighs.

The Wild Bee Valley was ablaze with flowers of various colors. Delong and Weila ventured into a world of blooms, where they were "besieged." Swayed by the breeze, tall chestnut and stone oak trees sprinkled jasmine and pink petals upon their heads and shoulders. The bushes known as Elsholtzia rugulosa rubbed purplish pollen on the cuffs of their sleeves with their dark grey branches covered with white fuzz. The mesmerizing fragrance of enumerable blossoms such as tatarian aster, orange day-lily, hypericum, and maguey agave infiltrated the cuffs on the loose legs of their pants.

But bees even outnumbered the flowers in the Wild Bee Valley. They buzzed up and down in the flowers. Some of them buried their heads sucking the nectar from the stamens of the flowers until their bellies were plump and glistened. Some were somersaulting on the petals and would not feel happy until their fuzzy hind legs were laden with pollen.

Delong and Weila were walking when suddenly a large swarm of bees buzzed over their heads like an airplane fleet.

Delong pulled Weila down to the ground in the thick grass, shouting, "Lie on your stomach. A bee swarm is coming!"

Pushing Delong's arm away, Weila raised his head out of the grass and looked forward with his wide-open eyes. He saw a large colony of bees skimming across the bushes like a golden mist drifting to the forest. Suddenly, the bees assembled and landed on the bough of a Chinese ash and formed a huge mass.

"Long-nosed Horse, what's going on here?" Weila asked Delong, his eyes blinking.

Weila had never kept bees before, so everything about bees was mystery to him. Delong, however, was different. As early as he started to have memory, his ama died of illness. Ada placed him in the care of Secretary Lang Shuai, with whom he had captured wild bees in the Wild Bee Valley.

Therefore, he knew everything about beekeeping.

Delong said, "This is a new colony separated from an original one. Look, how big a swarm it is!"

Clicking his tongue, Weila exclaimed, "How wonderful it would be if they flew into our log skeps! Then how happy Grandpa Enweng would be!"

Delong said, "Don't be anxious. Let's find out where they're going to settle down first."

Just then, the bees hanging from the tree came apart buzzing and flew forward after the queen bee, looking for an appropriate place to call their home.

"Fly to the apiary!" shouted Weila, waving his hand at the bee colony, "We'll treat you well!"

The swarm flew by a hawthorn grove and then over an expanse of grassland.

Above the grassland, there were two glittering silvery lines.

The silvery lines whistled in the mountain wind.

These are military telephone lines leading to the 179th Armory.

Delong knew how important these two lines were. They connected the military command post with the border sentry posts and the militia joint defense teams in all the border area villages. Delong had once delivered some muntjack jerky to ada in the armory. He scurried on the mountain path as joyous as a parrot. He soon covered a dozen kilometers and arrived. He had just entered when ada's telephone ran. Ada picked it up, but what Delong overheard was the buzz of a bee on the phone. But ada suddenly looked extremely grave, every wrinkle on his face burrowing as prominent as if they had been chiseled on a rock. The "buzz" was in fact not the sound of a bee but a call from the upper-level command post. It issued a warning of emergence against a band of bandits across the border who would come to rob the armory of its weapons. With the information, the troops began to prepare for an ambush. The command post told the armory to tighten its guard. During that eventful night, ada took some soldiers with him to go on patrol while more guards were posted to protect the armory. Delong shared a single bed with a platoon leader named Yang Jia, who wore a black, stubbly beard. Squeezed on the bed, none of them could go to sleep. Opening their eyes wide, they kept listening what was happening on the border. Soon, volleys of gunshots came from it. The battle was engaged. Delong sprang up on his bottom, saying, "Please let me go into battle with the troops." Platoon Leader Yang also sat up and responded, "If we could go, it'd better for me than for you. I'm so eager that my palms are sweating. But this is order. Order! Do you understand?" Delong kept nodding his head. He assumed that the guy who had given the order must have been a high-ranking commander. He can make everyone listen to him. If that's the case, it'd be no use pleading. *Anyone, neither of us can go, and both of us have to obey this high-ranking commander's orders.* The next day, ada told Delong, "The armory is an eyesore of the bandits on the other side of the order. After they failed to rob it, they'll find ways to sabotage it. We must be vigilant all the time. We mustn't allow the telephone lines to break for a second." Delong passed this information on to Weila and Ema. whenever they had spare time, the three children would follow the line-checking soldiers into dense forest along the telephone lines to check on them. When they found tree branches grow long enough for vines on them to climb onto the telephone posts, they would cut the branches off with their machetes to ensure that communication via the lines was unimpeded.

Then, Delong and Weila traced the bee colony to the telephone post.

Wow! The colony of bees kept flying until they reached the telephone lines, where they alighted somewhere between them and soon formed into a mass. Viewed from a distance, the phone lines seemed to have grown with a jackfruit berry. What was going on?

They took a closer look and found that a tree fork broken by the wind from a tree was caught between the two telephone lines and the bees tired from flying was taking a break in a gathering.

The tree fork and the swarm of bees weighed the telephone lines down so that they swayed glistening when there was wind.

*This won't do. What if the lines break?*

Weila pulled his machete out, cut off a small tree beside him, and whittled it into a stick. He was about to rush to the phone lines…

…when Delong held him by his clothes asking, "What're you doing?"

Wielding the stick, Weila responded, "I'll poke the bee mass off the tree fork!"

Delong yanked the stick from Weila's hand and reprimanded, "Are you crazy? Even bears that steal honey dare not offend a swarm of bees."

Weila said, "As soon as I poke, I'll run like mad. I'm sure the bees can't catch up with me."

Delong snorted, "It's the opposite. When you run, you'll create a gust of wind. Then the bees will trace the wind to you, and their stings will make you scream out loud."

"What?" Weila shook his head helplessly and asked, "What…what shall we do then?"

Delong was silent. He pulled a few yellow flowers and drew an arrow from his deerskin quiver. He tied the flowers to the arrow with some cogon grass, drew the bow, and swish, shot the arrow out.

The arrow decorated with the flowers landed right in the bee mass.

Buzz! The mass was startled and scattered.

Something strange happened: the startled and scattered bees did not fly randomly in all directions. On the contrary, together they chased the darting arrow into the distance.

Weila asked blinking, "What are the bees chasing the arrow for?"

Delong explained in reply, "When they're pushed over, they'll fight back! Their big eyes are most sensitive to the color yellow. When they found that something yellow was attacking them, they were determined not to let it go!"

Weila broke into a laughter, "Ha-ha! They're fooled this time!"

Delong stowed his bow.

"Let's go, Weila. Let's get the tree fork down."

Holding the stick high, Weila said, "I'll go and poke it down!"

"We can't poke it right under the phone lines. We may break them by doing so."

"Okay. I'll climb up the pole and lift the fork off the lines."

Holding the telephone pole with both arms and legs, Weila, shuffled, shuffled, and shuffled, and soon reached the top. "Hey, hand me the stick!"

Delong raised the stick high and handed it to Weila, who lifted the tree fork off the phone lines with care.

Delong said, "Bid-headed Horse, you need to become a giraffe now. Strain your neck and look into the distance and see if there're more forks on the phone lines, okay?"

"Okay!" After casting the stick, he placed his hand above his eyes and peered into the distance.

In the sunlight, the glistening silvery lines crossed the grassland and extended into the thick forest, where they were half visible from time to time through the foliage.

Suddenly, Weila widened his eyes…

Yikes! Something was flickering on the silvery lines, and it looked like a serrated sickle used to cut upland rice.

"Delong, something terrible is happening! Someone is sawing the lines!"

"What?" Upon hearing it, Delong drew an arrow out swiftly and asked in earnest, "Where? Where?"

"Just under the dragon fruit tree," shouted Weila as he slid down the post.

But when they rushed to the dragon fruit tree, bow and machete in hand, they were both dumbfounded...

No one was sawing the telephone lines.

It was but a sharp bamboo leaf stuck on the phone line, and it was covered with dewdrops all over.

When the bamboo leaf waved in the sunlight, the dewdrops glittered.

# Chapter 2

"What? You're going to capture wild bees in the valley?"

While chewing steamed glutinous rice, Grandpa Enweng kept sizing up the three children eating their breakfast with his eyes smiled into slits. He continued, "You're really a bunch of tireless skylarks. Yes, the Wild Bee Valley, the Wild Bee Valley. It's so called because it's full of wild bees. This early spring, a few colonies flew away from our apiary. Since I've been as busy as a bee, I haven't found time to capture them. I've been thinking of the old saying 'A pestle will always fall back into the mortar no matter how high it's lifted.' So, no matter how far the bees fly, they'll never get out of the Wild Bee Valley. I'll capture them all when I can find some helping hands in the future."

Ema chimed in, "Now you've got helping hands. After we capture the bees, we can also harvest lots of their honey. Then, with the honey we get from our apiary, we can bring more honey to the PLA uncles on the Army Day on August 1. Please let us go!" As she pleaded, she shook her grandpa by his leg, "You're a good grandpa. Please!"

Delong added, "Grandpa Enweng, don't worry about us. I used to capture wild bees with Secretary Lang Shuai. I know how to please them, so they won't attack my friends with their poisonous stings."

"He-he-he!" chuckled Grandpa Enweng. "Among the birds in the old-growth forest, only the parrots can talk glibly. But you talk more glibly than they are. Alright, this afternoon, you may go and try your luck. However, you mustn't go deeper in the forest. It's hard to say you won't run into bears or leopards. If you're unlucky, you may even come across long-haired monsters."

"Long-haired monsters?" Ema became nervous.

Grandpa Enweng withdrew his smile and said, "Long-haired monsters are the ghosts of the people killed by wild animals. They have long hairs all over, and their eyelashes are so long that they cover their eyes. They're tired of being ghosts in the forms of monsters in the old-growth forest, so they're looking for people venturing into it to take their place. If you should run into them, don't expect to come out of the forest this life."

"Gosh!" Ema unconsciously licked her lips. At the same time, she looked sideways at Delong and Weila to observe if they were scared of the long-haired monsters.

Delong was fishing out a boiled egg from the clay pot. While tossing it from hand to hand to cool it off, he said, "Long-haired monsters must like eating eggs. I'll take a couple to improve their life quality. Maybe, we're lucky enough to watch a long-haired monster fighting a water monster."

Weila cast a glance at Ema and suggested, "Ema, if you don't like to watch monsters fight each other, you'd better stay by the fire pit and cook for us. The food you fix is scrumptious."

"Yes, yes, I will go!" Looking into Grandpa Enweng's eyes, Ema grunted, "Grandpa, our teacher has told us that people won't become ghosts after they die."

Grandpa Enweng burst into a guffaw, "Ha-ha-ha! It means your grandpa is still stuck with the same old way of thinking, as old as a knot in an old tree. I'm still super-stitious, believing in gods, spirits, and ghosts, right? But capturing bees is a delicate work and also risky. If you were all as careless as Weila who mistook a bamboo leaf as a serrated sickle, then you can never be able to capture any bee. May the spirits of the dead be kind to you and bring you good luck this afternoon!"

At napping time, Ema was especially alert. Lying in the shack, she tossed and turned and could not shut her eyes no matter how she tried. Now, the cicadas began to sing with their high whining trill as if to say, "Arise...! Arise...!" Then, the mallards by the valley river started quacking. They quacked and quacked as if to say "Come to the valley! Come to the valley!" Straining her ears amid the hubbub of noises, she tried to distinguish if Delong and Weila were stirring in their shack. She was worried that they might sneak away without notifying her. Everyone knows how enticing venturing into the old-growth forest to capture wild bees was to someone like Ema who had never done so ever before. She found it as mysterious as intriguing. *What do wild bees look like? Are they happy to be captured and brought to the apiary? While bees are flying in the forest, how can we capture them?* She had so many questions that she got more and more confused. After a while, she became drowsy and gradually went to sleep. Perhaps a sleep-inducing bug mentioned in Grandpa Enweng's stories had sneaked into her ear and brought her to the dreamland.

Suddenly, a long-haired monster stormed into the shack and reached out its claws toward her…

"Ugh!" Ema was startled awake.

Then she heard Weila shouting with irritation, "What are you yelling for? What are you yelling for?"

Abashed, she grimaced, "Long-haired monster…"

Weila rolled his eyes and mimicked her "Ugh."

"We're going to capture wild bees. Stay here and go on fighting your long-haired monster!"

"Hey, hey! Wait for me!" Ema rolled up, picked up the small gourd filled with spring water, and rushed out of the shack to tag after them.

Delong and Weila had long been ready. They each held a log skep in their arms. Besides, Delong also carried a fully loaded cloth satchel over his shoulder.

Delong smiled at Ema, saying, "Fairy, did you dream of flying to heaven? If you're still enjoy yourself there, Big-headed Horse and I going ahead now."

"You're wrong. She was almost scared to death by a long-haired monster" cut in Weila!

"You're the long-haired monster!" retorted Ema as she fixed the small gourd water bottle to her waist and then made a face at Weila.

She asked Delong, "Can I carry a log skep?"

Delong shook his head, "You'd better be barehanded. It'd be more convenient for you to escape from the long-haired monster."

Ema snatched the satchel from Delong's shoulder and put it over hers.

"I'm not going to run for life," Ema snorted, "I'll see with my own eyes how you guys will be so scared that you'll crawl into your log skeps!"

Chatting and laughing, the three children were on their way to the Wild Bee Valley.

Delong walked in the front while Weila brought the rear, sandwiching Ema in the middle.

Delong worked hard to open the way by cutting off road-blocking vines and cogon grass.

Bringing the rear, Weila had equally a hard time. He had to stop from time to time to pat off jawed land leeches from the cuffs of his pants. Sensitive to commotion, the leeches fall from the blades of grass as people walk through it. The leeches would raise their head suckers and attach themselves to the shoes and pant cuffs of those who followed. Then, these creepy crawlies will wiggle slowly to a person's ankle, choose a proper location, and start sucking blood. They will not retract their head suckers until their stomach are so full that they will almost pop. Then, they will fall back into the grass. As he patted off the jawed land leeches, he yelled at them, "See if you can climb up again!" Whack! A leech was patted off. "See if you can climb up again!" Whack, another was patted off.

Sandwiched in the middle, Ema looked left and right and could not help feeling disappointed. Wild bees were not at all as many as he had expected. Here came one, and there came another. Without paying attention, she found it hard to even see them.

"I say, why aren't we walking toward where there are more flowers?" asked Weila in a complaining tone as he wiped sweat off his face. "Wild bees live on flower nectar instead of dew."

Ema also added, "Are wild bees still napping now?"

"Yes, they're also dreaming of long-haired monsters," Delong jeered with a chuckle. Patting Weila on his shoulder, he continued, "As there are both gold and sand in a river, so there are lots domestic and wild bees among flowers, but how can we tell them apart? To capture wild bees, we must go deeper in the forest, to where domesticated bees won't go."

Now Weila and Ema came to realize that to capture wild bees, we can't go to places where there are a lot of bees.

After they walked a long while, they came into a poorly lit teak grove. Looking up, they found the foliage blocking the sun; looking down, they saw their feet buried in decomposing leaves. The chilly wind was imbued with the smell of mildew and moist.

Delong stopped, put down his log skep, and said, "Let's catch wild bees here."

Ema opened her eyes wide and looked around in search of wild bees.

"Well, I can't even find a single one. What are we catching?"

Delong took the cloth satchel off her shoulder and said with a smile, "We'll find them. You and Weila go and hide in that grove, and I'll join you soon."

Weila and Ema took shelter in a grove of horseweed. Weila pulled the leafed branches apart and called to Delong, "Hey, we all depend on you. You're the one that eats the most anyway!"

"Ha-ha! Just keep your eyes wide open!"

Delong broke a branch off a tree, took out from his satchel a small bamboo tube filled with honey, and sprinkled some on the leaves. Then, he produced a piece of honeycomb, hung it to a tree with a string, struck a match, and set fire to it. As the honeycomb burned, it sent forth clouds of dark smoke, which, imbued with the sweetness of honey, began to permeate the forest. It spread and spread...

Carrying the satchel in his hand, Delong came to the horseweed grove. He said to Weila and Ema, "Can you all smell it! It's intoxicating and will work wonders. Wild bees will fly over soon. After they collect the nectar, they'll fly back to their nest. Then, we can trace them to it and capture them."

Delong had hardly finished when Ema blurted out, "Look! Look! Bees are coming!"

Sure enough! A few wild bees had arrived from no one knows where. They buzzed around the leaves sprinkled with honey. Soon, a big-bellied bee alighted on it and started sucking the nectar. Soon after that, a few other bees descended and sucked the honey on the flowers greedily. The big-bellied bee had stuffed with the honey, took off buzzing, and circled around the branch two times.

Weila sprang up, saying, "Hurry. The big-bellied bee is going to fly away! Let's go after it."

Delong pressed him down, saying, "Don't be anxious. Listen carefully before you go."

The big-bellied bee flew up in a high speed while buzzing in a high pitch.

"Listen, it buzzes so sharply. It's far away from its nest," said Delong, who fixed his eyes on the wild bees indulging in a sucking feast on the leaves. He continued, "We need to listen and find those whose buzz will tell us that their nest is close to us. They buzz in a deep, slow humming tone with a drawl like this…" As he said so, he began to mimic the sound while pinching his nose.

Ema said, "I see! It's like a plane!"

Weila objected, "Nah! It's a bear farting!"

They joked and laughed for a while before they quieted down. Straining their ears, they began to identify the buzzing sound of the wild bees.

Humming! Buzzing! Before the bees on the branch left, a few other bees came from the forest. Suddenly, the sound changed. It was neither buzzing nor humming. Instead, it sounded like shuffling. It sounded like something big coming out of the depth of the old-growth forest, brushing tree branches and trampling fallen leaves.

The horrifying sound gave the children a gnawing feeling. Shuffling, shuffling...

Ah! A monster-like creature presented itself from behind the trees. It was covered with long hair all over.

"A long-haired monster! A long-haired monster!" exclaimed Ema with alarm.

Delong quickly put his hand over Ema's mouth and warned, "Be quiet! Don't you want to live?"

Ema was so scared that she opened her eyes wide and grasped, grasping Delong tight by his arm.

Weila quietly drew out his machete and, poking Delong in his waist, said in a hushed voice, "It's a bear."

Weila was right. It was a big-headed bear waddling out of the thickets. It held its neck up and looked around with his gem-like dark eyes while wriggling his nose to sniff. Then it opened its long muzzle and bared its two rows of white teeth, with slimy saliva streaming out of its mouth. The bear walked slowly to the branch covered with honey, stood up, and swatted away the bees with his paw. Then it sat down, held the branch in its paws, and began chewing it.

Honey is the bear's favorite. A bear is often stung and bruised badly while stealing it.

Weila whispered in Delong's ear, "Our log skep is too small for it!"

Delong shook his head, "I didn't expect to run into a bear."

Ema said, "Let's run for our lives. Gee, my legs gave way beneath me!"

Indeed, her legs gave way so much that she could not stand up on her feet.

Delong tilted his head and gave the order, "Let's pull out!"

The children were in no mood to catch wild bees. They even forgot to take their log skeps with them as they took flight. They ran and ran, leaving the bear far behind, leaving the grass far behind, and leaving the forest far behind. They headed straight for the bamboo forest. Suddenly, Delong slipped and fell thumping and splashing to the muddy ground, getting smeared all over.

It turned out that they approached a pool.

Weila dipped his finger into the water and stuck his tongue out to lick it and said, "Hey, it's kind of salty."

Delong said, "This pool will help us a lot. Those who come here to get water are old bees that can't fly far away.

Their nest is just close by. We'll find it, mark it, and come back to catch them tomorrow."

As he was speaking, an old bee came buzzing and alighted by the pool. It crawled tentatively forward and extended its tongue into the water. Soon, it had enough. It took off buzzing with a drawl, its long belly laden with salty water.

"Go after it!" Delong gave his command.

"Charge!" shouted Weila running in the front while wielding his machete. Focusing on the chase, he tripped over a vine lying in the grass. He rolled a couple of times and pushed Delong away when the latter tried to help him up in a hurry. Laughing at himself, he said to Delong, "Go ahead and chase the bee. This Big-headed Horse was taking a sand bath. My wallowing was graceful, wasn't it?"

Delong nodded while running, "Yes, it was graceful! Graceful! I'd like to take a sand bath if I were not in a hurry to run after the old bee!"

Ema gasped aloud, "Delong! Weila! You guys had better open your eyes wide. I can't see clearly because sweat keeps running into my eyes. I can't see things clearly. It's all up to you guys…"

The old bee was flying and flying, and the children were chasing and chasing.

The old bee flew out of the forest. As it passed by an electricity pole, it sped up. In the blink of an eye, it became a dot as small as a soybean and disappeared in the forest.

"Where's the old bee?" Delong stopped to ask Weila.

Weila responded shrugging, "It's vanished!"

"We've already come this far. Maybe the bee nest is just close by. Let's spread out and look for it," said Delong.

Weila said, "Are we looking for a needle in a haystack?"

"Of course, it's no easy job," said Delong, who bent over, pulled off a grass blade, and, holding it close to Weila and Ema, said, "Take a look and see what it is."

Weila said, "Something that cows like to eat."

Seeing some yellowish stains on the blade, Ema blurted out in surprise, "Bee poop! It's bee poop! The bee nest is just nearby!"

Rolling his eyes, Weila asked, "How do you know?"

"Well," Ema said drawling intentionally, "Of course, I know! That's because I do cleaning at the apiary every day. Grandpa told me that when bees come in and out of the hives, they always poop at the entrances. Bee poop means the bee nest is not far away anymore."

"Let's go and find it!" said Weila, who immediately felt excited.

So, the three children started searching in three directions with their eyes wide open. Delong found some bee poop on a broad alocasia leaf. Ema also spotted bee poop on a baccaurea leaf. Weila found it in the grass under a telephone pole.

"Wow! Here is a large buildup of bee poop. It may be from a queen bee," shouted Weila.

Both Gelong and Ema gathered around to take a look.

"Well, it's not bee poop," giggled Ema. "It's a pile of bird's poop!"

"Let me see what it is," said Delong. He picked up a little bit, rubbed it between his fingers gently, and put it close to his nose. After he sniffed at it, he said, "It's not bee poop. It's saw dust!"

"Saw dust?" Ema asked wide-eyed.

"Yea, it's the dust of wood when it was sawed."

"Strange! Where did it come from?"

As he mumbled, Weila looked up at the telephone pole.

This was a pole of pine wood, straight and smooth, standing tall on a precipitous crag. It was especially thick probably because of its strategic and inaccessible location. The two crossarms on the top were extremely thick as well. The silvery lines extended to the thick forest in the distance through the porcelain insulators on the crossarms.

Halfway on the pole there was a serial number 109 marked clearly with white paint.

Delong raked his eyes over the pole from the top to the base, but he did not find any damage.

The base of the pole was buried deep in the grass. Delong separated the grass blades with his hand and found the part close to the ground was encircled with mud.

He pulled down a piece of the mud…

What?!

Beneath the mud, there was a saw mark.

"Someone has sawed the pole!" exclaimed Ema and Weila in chorus.

Yes, someone sawed the pole!

The saw mark was very deep, cutting into more than half of the pole!

If this thick power pole were sawed down, it would pull the telephone lines into several sections!

"Who's so audacious!" Weila was so angry that he pulled out his glinting machete again.

"This hooligan was trying to sabotage the telephone pole. Why didn't he saw it down?" asked Ema.

Delong nodding, "You're right! Why didn't he saw it through? Did he want a big gust of wind to blow it down? Or did he want a wild boar to push it down while rubbing against it to relieve its itching?"

Weila said, "Hey, he must have decided to cut it down. But we scared him away when he heard us coming!"

"Nope!" said Delong as he rubbed the mud in his fingers, "The mud pasted around the pole is already dried up. This son of a gun has long gone. We must report it immediately!"

Ema said, "Yes, we must report it to Secretary Lang Shuai and the veteran Production Leader Ka Bure.

Weila said, "If we're going to report it, we must report it to the PLA uncles first!"

Casting a glance at the silvery lines, Ema said, "If only we had a telephone. Like Uncle Line-inspector Xiao, we can use iron clips to connect the phone with the phone lines. Then we can report it right away!"

The "Line-inspector Xiao" that Ema mentioned was Uncle Xiao Lun, a telephone technician working in the

179th Armory. He was making inspection tours along the telephone lines every day, with spare lines around his neck, a submachine gun over his shoulder, and a stand-alone device and climbing boards in his waist belt. Swoosh, swoosh, swoosh! He patrolled back and forth like an arrow. When asked where he was going, his answer was always, "To inspect the lines!" Naturally, he became known by his nickname "Line-inspector Xiao."

With regard to Ema's reference to a telephone, Weila also shouted, "Yes, how wonderful it would be if we had one!" While he said so, he pressed his machete blade against his ear and spoke into it as if it were the receiver of a telephone, "Hello! Hello! This is Weila speaking. I'd like to talk to Company Commander Mu Sade...!"

He had barely finished speaking when Company Commander Mu Sade answered in person from the thick forest—a scenario that would only happen in fairytales.

"This is Mu Sade. Please tell me what you're going to say. But you've got to be careful about your ears!"

The three children directed their eyes toward where the voice came from all together, and what they saw made them beside themselves with joy.

Out from the forest there came three PLA uncles, with Mu Sade in the lead.

Following him was Platoon Leader Yang and "Line-inspector Xiao."

The children shouted and jumped, reaching out their arms like birds spreading their wings.

The sweaty body odor of Mu Sade told Delong that ada and the other two uncles had been patrolling the Wild Bee Valley border for a long time. The company stationed in the 179th Armory was a reinforced one, with two platoons guarding the armory and two scattering in different sentry posts. Mu Sade often led a patrolling detachment to inspect boundary markers and telephone lines. It took them over a week to finish each round. This time, the detachment had just patrolled three days when he got the phone call from the command post. After he hung up, he sent for Platoon Leader Yang and Line-inspector Xiao, and they set out to return to the armory. Sensing that something was weighing on Company Commander's mind on their way, Platoon Yang knew without asking that something urgent had happened. Eventually, however, he could not help asking, "Is the 179th Armory being targeted again?" Mu Sade nodded. "Like the fish that can't be concealed by the whirlpools in the Wild Bee Valley river, the bandits on the other side of the border are ready to make trouble again: They've planned to blow up the armory after they failed to rob it. They'll deliver bombs across the border after midnight tomorrow to their associates on our side.

They had not expected to run into Delong and his friends.

"Ada, someone has sawed the telephone pole!"

"What?"

When they came to the pole No.109, the sight enraged "Line-inspector Xiao". He screamed, "Who did this? I'll shoot and kill him when I catch him!"

Mu Sade asked, "Children, tell me how you discovered this? Did you see it as soon as you got to the pole?"

Delong picked up the mud that he had broken into pieces from the ground.

"Ada, they were originally pasted around the part of the pole that had been sawed. When we first came, we found the pole alright. We detected the saw mark after we lifted a piece of the mud off it."

Mu Sade nodded, "This is what it got to be: Whoever sawed the pole would not forget to cover it up with the mud."

Platoon Leader Yang said, "They did not saw the pole down completely because it's not the time for it to be toppled yet."

"You're completely correct. When the time comes, someone only needs to give it a gentle push, snap! our communication would be cut off."

While speaking, Mu Sade took the mud pieces from Delong, sprinkled some of the water from Ema's gourd bottle, and after softening the mud pieces, pasted it back to the saw mark on the pole.

As he was plastering the pole, he said to the children beaming, "You guys are great! Your eagle eyes are as sharp as knives. But remember, if we weed the area around a burrow, the sly rabbit would never return to it!"

"Now I understand!" Delong said, "We mustn't alert the bad guys who sawed the pole if we want to catch them."

"That's right!" responded Mu Sade, running his loving hand over his son's head.

Delong asked, "Why did he saw the pole? Just for purpose of sabotage?"

Ema added, "That's my question, too. Why did they attempt the sabotage?"

Mu Sade replied, "The only thing I can tell you all is that all their sabotage attempts are aimed at the 179th Armory, which has weapons and ammunition. The bandits entrenched in the border area see it as their greatest threat and thus an eyesore. They want to rob it, but if they find it impossible, they'll sabotage it."

Holding his machete up, Weila said, "Uncle Mu Sade, tell us what we can do to protect the armory. Just give us orders!"

Patting the children on their shoulders, Mu Sade said, "What you should do at this point is do a good job in helping Grandpa Enweng with his beekeeping work. You want to catch wild bees, right? That's great! Increase your bee colonies to generate more wealth for the villagers. It's a good deed to do. While taking care of the bees, you must do your homework assigned by your teachers. I'll find time to check on you guys. If you fail to finish your home assignments, mind your ears!" As he said so, he pulled Weila at his ear gently to demonstrate his warning.

Weila was anxious, "What about the telephone poles? What about the armory?"

Mu Sade pulled the three children into his arms and, blinking his eyes mysteriously, said, "As for this incident, just pretend that you have seen or heard nothing. And when the next time you come to catch wild bees, don't come near to this No.109 pole.'

"What!" the children were all confused after hearing this.

Platoon Yang picked up Mu Sade's topic and continued, "Yes, treat this incident as a rice cake. Stuff it in your mouth and let it digest in your stomach. Don't tell anyone. Do you understand?"

Weila patted himself on his big head and exclaimed, "Jeez, this is too complicated. Ema, do you have your sewing kit with you?"

Ema shook her head apologetically, "No, I don't have it. What do you need that for?"

"I'll sew my mouth up!"

# Chapter 3

It was easy said than done.

The incident of the pole being sawed was not as easily chewed and digested as a rice cake. As soon as they returned to the apiary, Weila told Grandpa Enweng about it before the other two children. Ema also added, "Uncle Mu Sade told us not to tell anyone!"

"Luckily, you have only me in the apiary. If bad guys heard about it, they would defeat your Uncle Mu Sade's plan! So, I must reprimand you. A red junglefowl hen never allows a snake to know her brooding nest. How could you let out so easily the parrot that Uncle Mu Sade asked you to cage?"

A glimmer of unusual graveness shone in Grandpa Enweng's otherwise smiling eyes.

"Grandpa, but you aren't a snake!" said Ema, her eyes twinkling.

Weila nodded his agreement, "Grandpa Enweng, I told you because you're a good guy."

"He-he-he!" Grandpa Enweng chuckled, "My children, you're as straightforward as an arrow. Children, you must remember this: Poisonous mushrooms and edible mushrooms can grow together in the same thick growth of grass; bad guys can always mingle themselves with good ones."

Delong said, "Weila, Ema, let's apologize. Grandpa is right. Let's make a vow to heavens that we won't tell about the pole to anyone else."

"Okay!" responded Weila and Ema in chorus.

"That's right, my children," said Grandpa Enweng, patting Delong with affection. "It's always good to correct a mistake that you've made. Uncle Mu Sade would commend you if he should learn about what you've done. It's okay now. The moon is pretty high. Go to sleep in your shacks. You worked the whole day without catching a wild bee. You'd better not go tomorrow so that I don't have to worry."

Delong pleaded, "Grandpa Enweng, please let us go. We didn't catch any bees because they flew too fast. We didn't catch up."

Grandpa Enweng laughed, "The sun still rises in the east tomorrow, and the wild bees will fly as fast."

"We've got a good idea, grandpa," Ema cried out. "Please let us go!"

Grandpa Enweng asked, "What's your good idea?"

Weila was the first to answer, "We promised to keep it a secret!"

A laugh broke through Grandpa Enweng's lips, "Look at you! You give away secrets when you're not supposed to! Alright, alright, I'm not going to ask anymore. If you still can't catch bees, I won't let you go any longer!"

"Deal!" agreed Delong.

The next day, the three children went into the Wild Bee Valley again.

They first arrived at the place where they ran into the bear yesterday, only to find the two log skeps they had left behind still lying there intact. Delong and Weila each scooped one and carried it on their shoulders. The three children then went deeper into the forest.

They walked and walked and finally found their way to the small pool of salt water.

It lay quietly in the thick grass.

An old bee came to water after a little while.

Weila raised the butterfly net and was about to flip it over the bee…

…when Delong stopped him, "Hold your horses! Wait till it gets enough water."

Ema chimed in, "Yes, it won't get back to its net before it draws enough water."

So, six eyes were fixed on the old bee at the same time.

Before long, the old bee had its full. It was about to take off when Weila rushed to it, raised the net, and swooped after it.

The old bee buzzed and bumped around in the net.

Delong reached his hand into the net and gently held it by its wings in his fingers.

"Ema, hurry and tie a silk thread to it!"

Ema produced a small piece of silk, from which she pulled a silk thread, made a loop, and put it around the old bee's abdomen.

"Delong, let it fly!"

Delong let go the old bee.

It took to the air dragging the silk thread.

As big as a thumbnail, the silk thread was carried by the old bee into the air.

It was such fun!

The old bee was flying and flying, the white silk thread was floating and floating, and the children were running and running.

The old bee stopped before a crag and descended.

There was a crack at the base of the crag, and bees flew in and out of it!

"Wow! We've found the old bee's nest!" exclaimed Weila jumping with joy.

Delong said to Weila, "Don't dance yet. Stop up the crack with mud quickly." And to Ema, "Go and tear off a banana leaf." Then, he produced a few pieces of honeycomb from his satchel, opened the back cap of the log skep, and placed them into it along with some sprinkles of honey.

At the same time, Weila had gotten some watery mud ready while Ema was back with a banana leaf.

Delong sealed the crack with the mud, leaving only a small hole. He rolled the banana leaf into a tube and inserted one end into the hole and the other end into the opening of the log skep, thus connecting it with the bee nest. After he finished, he wiped off the sweat off his face and proclaimed, "Let's wait and see. The wild bees are going to relocate!"

The sealing of the crack with the watery mud caused confusion and buzzing commotion in the colony. Suddenly, their attention was caught by the aroma of the honey in the banana-leaf tube. Several workers went into it, only to find a new home with honey readily available. They went back and escorted the queen bee into the log skep.

Then, the log skep became lively inside.

Ema said to the bees remaining in the crack, "Sweethearts, we'll bring you to the best home you can find. You don't have to be wild and live a hard life in the old-growth forest anymore."

The wild bees vied with one another in entering the skep, as if they had understood her cajoling words.

Buzzing! Buzzing! The skep became increasingly bustling and lively.

After a while, the whole colony had found their way into the log skep.

Weila was so happy that he rolled on the grassy ground. As if that was not enough to express his joy, he stood upside down and began to "walk" on his hands. He had just taken two "steps" when he paused, fixing his eyes on something in the distance.

Delong asked, "Why did you stop?"

"I saw a bear on the dragon-fruit tree!" With a somer-sault, Weila stood on his feet. Placing his hand above his eyes and kept crying out, "Look there! A bear was picking the dragon fruit and eating it."

"What?" Eyes widening, Ema suggested to Delong, "We'd better run before it comes to ask us of our honey."

"Of course," responded Delong while plugging the opening of the skep tight. "Big-headed Horse, where's the bear?"

"Just over there!"

Delong squinted his eyes and peered into the direction that Weila was pointing. He saw in the distance a grayish white branch of a dragon fruit tree sticking out of a thick grove. He scanned the trunk of the tree and focused his eyes on a flickering shadow. Delong gazed more intently for a little while and cried out suddenly, "Yikes, it's not a bear. It's a man!"

"How can a man covered with long, black hair all over," questioned Weila, his eyes turning big and round.

"Eek! Can it be a long-haired monster?" Ema panicked.

"That's not black hair, but a black blanket!" asserted Delong.

Rubbing his eyes, Weila took another look. Sure enough, it was a wobbling dark human figure, a man with a black blanket draping from his head.

The black blanket covered the man from his head to his knee.

Elderly people from the Menglang Mountain Village all liked to cover their heads with a blanket as this man did when they went into the forest or the valley. They did so to shield themselves from dewdrops, which they believed would get them sick if they were exposed to it.

After observing for another moment, he suddenly caught sight of a telephone line running under the dragon fruit tree. It instantly reminded him of the pole nearly sawed down.

"There're telephone lines under the tree. What is he doing on the tree?" Delong asked himself. "Let's go and take a look. Leave the skeps here for the time being, and we'll get them afterwards."

The three children waded through the tall grass toward the dragon fruit tree.

They were walking gingerly when Ema screamed in a hushed voice, "Hey, look! The man's climbing down the tree!"

Sure enough! Through the thick grass blades, they saw a man covered with a black blanket clambered down the dragon fruit tree.

When the children arrived under the tree, the man with the black blanket was nowhere to be found.

The tall dragon fruit tree laden with the berries stood silently above the grass.

It was flanked by a camphor tree on the right and a telephone pole on the left in a short distance. Silvery lines ran on the crossarms and led to the old-growth forest. Argyreia obtusifolia, or "silver-backed," vines were enlacing both the trees, their countless brownish arms of various thickness intertwining themselves into a huge mesh to ensnare their two host trees of great stature. The grayish white trunk of the dragon fruit tree was also infested with parasitic plants. From time to time, ripe dragon-fruit berries were swept off the tree by the wind and fell into the thick growth of grass.

Delong sized the dragon fruit tree up and down, murmuring to himself, "Why did he climb up the tree?"

Just then, something under the tree caught his eye: on an oblate grass blade there were a few drops of fluid of reddish brown. They looked like blood.

Well, was he bleeding?

Delong soon figured out that the fluid was not blood. But it was sap seeping out of a broken "silver-backed" vine, which he finally located amid the entangled mesh. What he saw gave him a shudder...

This "silver-backed" vine came from a crotch of the tall dragon fruit tree and hung diagonally down to the base of the camphor tree. Running beneath thick vine leaves, it seemed to have entered the ground at first look. However, when he raked the vine leaves apart with his hands, he found the arm-thick vine did not enter the ground, but was cut off. Coiling around the camphor tree a few times like a python, it was tied by its end into a fast knot tied firmly to the bottom part of the trunk. Crimson sap was still seeping from the cut of the "silver-backed" vine. Delong ran his eyes along the vine that led up to the crotch to the other side and slanted down, where it was fastened in the same fashion to a big bough pointing to the west.

*What's the purpose?*

*Why did the man with a black blanket coiled the vine around the two trees?*

Delong decided to climb up the dragon fruit tree to take a look.

Now, everything was clear to him…

The bough pointing to the west was barely sawed off. It could have broken off if it had not been pulled by the "silver-backed" vine. And the glistening silvery lines were just running underneath this crotch. When needed, severing the "silver-backed" vine under the camphor tree with a single cut would topple the sawed bough, which would fall and break the telephone lines, thus discontinuing all the military communication.

Aah! Delong gazed with astonishment at the deep saw mark in the crotch of the tall tree.

Suddenly, he saw in his mind's eye the big crotch turning into the erect telephone pole; the grayish white spots on the bark transforming into No.109, the white paint serial number on the pole; and the shadow of the foliage, changing into a man covered with a black blanket…

Yes, it's him! It's this villain!

*He sawed the telephone pole and now came to saw the dragon fruit tree!*

Pulling the leaves apart in front of him, he caught a vague sight of a figure covered with a black blanket wobbling on the path leading to the Menglang Mountain Village through the forest.

*Aha, this villain hasn't gone far yet!*

Delong was burning with wrath.

Clambering down the dragon fruit tree as fast as he could, he told Weila and Ema this startling discovery.

"What?" Weila and Ema exclaimed, "Let's go and catch him!"

Like three flying arrows or three little swimming fish, the three children sped to the path through the forest to run after the blanket-covered man.

They ran and ran, throwing the trees back and leaving their footprints behind, their sweat splashing on the grass blades.

They ran and ran when a large tract of man-high devil weed blocked their way.

In the thicket on the other side of the devil weed flashed the blanket-covered man.

Delong whispered like a mosquito, "My ada told us not to startle a bad guy. I suggest we shadowing him instead of capturing him…"

"Yes!" Ema nodded, "We'll find out who he is, where he is going, and what other sabotage activities he's going to engage in. When we have figured out everything, we'll report it to your ada!"

Weila shrugged, "The vote is two to one. Your proposal's passed."

The devil weed blocked their way like a wall, so thick that even a rabbit could hardly get in. Hunters had cut a narrow path through it. Apparently, the blanket-covered man had found his way to the thicket through his path. The three children followed him to this only route leading to the other side. The path led to great depths. Walking along it, they could see nothing but the devil weed around them. They walked and walked and finally approached the other end, when, all of a sudden, they heard footsteps coming toward them…

Swishy! Swashy!

It seemed that someone was wading across the thick grass toward them.

*Who is it? Could the blanket-covered man turn around to follow us when he sensed that we've been trailing him?*

Delong removed his crossbow from his back, Weila pulled out his machete from his waist, and Ema took cover behind Weila, grabbing him by his shirt.

Swishy! Swashy! Swishy! Swashy!

The footsteps were coming closer and louder to the exit.

The three children looked back. The route of retreat was too far away to give them enough time to flee. They looked left and right, but the devil weed was too thick to get in. Focusing their eyes on the narrow exit, they were waiting for anything unexpected to happen, ready to fight a life-and-death battle.

However, silence fell after a moment.

*What's going on? The blanket-covered man paused?*

Delong pricked his ears to listen, but he heard nothing stirring.

He thought a little and said, "Weila, you and Ema stay put. I'll go ahead and take a look!"

Widening his eyes, Weila said, "Do you think I'm not good enough? I should go ahead of you."

"Okay!" Delong had to give his consent.

The two sneaked to the exit, where they leaned against the devil weed on both sides and, pulling the leaves apart, looked. But they gasped at the sight:

An adult bear was standing on the grass like a giant!

The bear might be figuring out which way to proceed or simply enjoying the view of the landscape. But the reality was that it was standing erect, its two hairy paws held chest high.

"Darn! The bear is on guard here!" Delong pouted his lips at Weila, "looks like it won't let us go without our passes."

Weila directed his eyes at the thicket far ahead and saw the blanket-covered man walking into the distance. He was anxious, "Jeez, the bad guy is escaping. It's impossible to catch up with him. What shall we do. This darned old bear. Why is it always crossing us all the time?"

Just then, Delong felt someone tugging at his shirt. He turned around, only to find Ema.

Ema had plucked up enough courage to sneak up.

Winking at Delong, she demanded, "Shoot your arrow. Hurry and shoot!"

Before Delong responded, Weila cut in, "Then, we're all going to die. The bear's skin is too thick to be penetrated even by the projectile of a blunderbuss. A struck by an arrow is just as good as a sting by a mosquito. It could only enrage the beast. With hair standing on end, it wouldn't give up chasing until it caught you!"

Just then, the bear turned half way around and started rubbing his side against a tree to release itching. Then, he rolled a bit on the grassy ground. When it finished, it headed toward the children.

Gosh! It seemed that the bear also wanted to go through the devil grass along the path.

What could the children do? Once it came to the exit, it would run into them.

Wishy! Washy! Wishy! Washy!

While the bear was drawing near, the three children held their breath, cold sweat breaking out on their foreheads.

"Let's charge against it," said Weila, who could no longer keep calm. "I'll take the lead!"

"No!" Delong pressed him down, his eyes still fixed on the oncoming bear. "Weila, Ema, it seems that we have to part company. When you rush out, you must catch up with the blanket-covered man. Remember, never startle him. Just shadow him and see which village he's from and what his's up to!"

"What about you, Delong?" asked Weila alarmed.

"I'll lead the bear away and catch up with you guys." When he finished, he pulled an arrow from his quiver and placed it on the crossbow. "We've no other alternative. I must lead it away!"

"Delong, it's too dangerous for you to do so!" said Weila while dragging Delong by his sleeve."

"Don't worry about me! Go and follow that villain!" Delong pulled his arm from Weila's hand. Rip! The sleeve was torn.

Delong dashed out of the devil weed and stood face to face with the bear.

His sudden appearance took the bear by surprise. It opened its mouth and roared. Sticking out its blood-red tongue, it assumed a pouncing posture. Delong pulled the bow and shot at the bear's forehead and hit its ear. Growl! The bear was enraged. Lifting his front paw, it brushed the arrow off its ear and threw itself upon Delong. The latter cast his crossbow and ran toward the forest. The bear scampered after him.

Delong darted into the thick forest soon, with the bear hot on his trail…

After Delong led the bear away, Weila and Ema dashed out of the devil weed and headed straight toward the thicket ahead.

Suddenly, Weila's eyes shone. He nudged Ema on her arm and pointed to the front, "Over there!'

Ema trained her eyes in the direction where Weila pointed. Sure enough, she saw a man covered with a black blanket walking unhurriedly. He seemed to be looking for something in the grass.

Weila and Ema went after him. They had followed for a short distance when the man came to a stop. Then, he crouched down and squatted there for a long time without the intention of standing up.

"What is he doing crouching there?" Ema asked Weila.

"He's pooping."

"Pooping? Well, it's possible."

The two children watched patiently for a long time. But the man with the black blanket was still crouching there motionless.

Weila could hardly wait, "How come it takes him such a long time to poop? Let's go and find out." With that, he rose.

Ema pulled him down and said in an admonishing tone "Don't move. Remember what Delong told us?"

Weila sighed and mumbled quietly, "Well, it makes me so anxious!"

Holding their temper, the two children waited for a few more minutes. But the man with the blanket still would not rise to his feet.

Weila's patience finally ran out. He stood up abruptly while pulling his machete out. "No, I can wait anymore!"

Ema tried to pull him but in vain. Weila charged forward in anger, wielding his machete.

Weila pussyfooted toward the man with the black blanket squatting on the grassy ground. He slowed down his pace as he approached him.

Holding his machete tight, he fixed his eyes on the man with a blanket, ready to fight him hard as soon as he turned around. But the man remained nonresponsive even when he stood right behind.

Just then, a sense of regret seized Weila.

Well, I'm not supposed to startle him.

But it was too late. Besides, there was no time for hesitation.

Weila took a big step forward, pulled the black blanket off that man's head, and, holding his machete high, shouted, "Don't move!"

The man whose blanket had been pulled off had a pair of ears shriveled like the wings of a bat. When the ear turned slightly around, a face presented itself to Weila. It was an old man's face covered with throbbing veins. The slender nose bridge on it was as pruned as his ears. Wrinkles were deeply and disorderly furrowed on his forehead, coupled with the immaturely grayed hair, made him look older than his age. The two deeply sunken eyes, however, were beaming daggers.

"Ahh!" Weila was taken aback at the sight of this face.

Ema also exclaimed with alarm.

The man with the black blanket was none other than the veteran Production Team Leader Ka Bure!

In his hands was a Chinese medicinal herb known as glossy ganoderma.

# Chapter 4

While Weila and Ema found the man with a blanket to be the veteran Production Team Leader Ka Bure, their friend Delong was still struggling with the bear.

Delong was leading the bear into the forest when, all of a sudden, he was tripped over a vine in the grass. Before he picked himself up, a looming shadow was pouncing upon him from behind bringing with it a gust of chilling wind imbued with the fishy odor of a wild animal.

Delong immediately rolled over on the ground to dodge the onslaught of the bear.

Failing to get its target, the bear turned around only to find Delong not there anymore.

Wonder where he was? He was on a sweet osmanthus tree now.

Holding the sweet osmanthus tree, the bear stood up abruptly. It reached its front paw to grab Delong's shoe. Pressing himself on the bough as close as he could, Delong wiggled his angle to shake off the shoe. With a bare foot, he was clambering up the tree with great effort.

The bear got hold of the shoe and raised it to its nose to sniff it. The odor assailed its nostrils and enraged it. As it grunted, it looked up and saw Delong climbing higher and higher, its little, round eyes gleaming with murder. Holding the shoe under its arm, it began to clamber up the tree. But when it reached out its front paw, the shoe dropped from its armpit.

An expert tree climber, the bear pulled itself up awkwardly and yet steadily with its limbs moving alternately. As it climbed, it glanced at Delong up above from time to time. As Delong had just passed the waist of the tree, the bear was up there, too. As Delong had climbed beyond the crotch, the bear also reached it.

Delong looked back, only to find the bear closing in. He looked around but found nothing that he could grasp. When he raised his head, he caught sight of an aerial root hanging from the midair.

This aerial root was hanging down from a Ficus hookeriana Corner tree. If he could get hold of it, he could swing to that tree.

But the aerial root was too far to reach with his hand. To climb further, the branches were too delicate. *What shall I do?*

He was fumbling about himself for something in panic when he touched the honeycomb knife in his waist.

A flash of joy lighted his eyes: An idea had dawned upon. He pulled the knife out and set to chop a long branch. He chopped and chopped until it was broken. He hurriedly lifted the branch to hook the aerial root with the tip where there was a branchlet. The branch was just long enough to reach the aerial root. Unfortunately, the branchlet pointed the same direction as the tip of the branch did. So, every time he got hold of the aerial root with the "hook" and tried to pull the main branch back, the aerial root would slip away. He tried two more times, and twice did he fail. He looked down and found the bear climbing closer and closer. He could even see clearly the black whiskers around its muzzle.

The bear could sweep Delong off the ground from the tree with a single slap of its paw if it had climbed up.

Delong was so anxious that sweat broke on the tip of his nose.

He raised his head and looked at the aerial root hanging in the midair. It was swaying as it slipped away from the branch and its branchlet. The sway instantly gave Delong an idea. He quickly reached the branch as far as he could and placed the "hook" against the root. Then he pushed it the other way with all his strength. Soon, the root swung back toward him.

Delong was about to grab the aerial root when the bear climbed up panting.

He hastily jabbed the bear with the tip of the branch. The bear growled and swiped the branch off Delong's hand. Then it reached its paw further trying to seize Delong. At the critical moment, the aerial root that had swung away now swayed back. Delong leapt up and snatched it. He then pushed himself away with his foot on the sweet osmanthus tree. Whoosh! He flew away from the bear's swiping paw like a nimble swallow and alighted on the Ficus hookeriana Corner tree. Delong let go the aerial root and held the tree tight.

Whack! The aerial root that had swung back hit the bear right in its face. Growl! Bursting into a fury, the bear pulled the aerial root off with its paw and crawled back from the sweet osmanthus tree. It had just backed to the middle of the trunk when all its paws loosened their grip and dropped to the ground with a thump. It rolled up, bared its teeth, and threw itself at the Ficus hookeriana Corner tree.

Seeing the bear ready to climb up this tree again, Delong scratched his head out of anxiety. He looked up to search for something that could help him out of the situation. Suddenly, he grinned from ear to ear...

Another aerial root was hanging above his head. It had a thick mass of wild bees as big as a calabash gourd.

*Yes, I got it!*

Delong climbed cautiously up to the other side of the bees and squatted on the crotch like a monkey.

Just then, the bear began clambering up puffing and blowing. He climbed and raised its blackish head to glance at Delong alternately.

When the bear was looking up, Delong seized the chance and cut off the aerial root with the bees on it.

The swarm of bees fell right on the bear's face.

Buzzing, buzzing! The bees flew apart in fright.

Countless bees rallied around and besieged the bear.

The bear tried to swat the bees with its front paws in a rush. The enraged bees began to attack the bear with their poisonous stings. Growl…growl… The bear was so painful that it fell off the tree, thumped to the ground, and made off into the old-growth forest swiftly.

The bear fled with the bees on its trail. Seizing this opportunity, Delong climbed down the tree.

He located his shoe in the grass, put it on, and ran away.

*Where to?*

*Back to Weila and Ema? But who knows where they are now?*

It's pretty close to the Menglang Mountain Village from here. Okay, I'd better return to the village and report everything to Secretary Lang Shuai. In case he's not there, I'll report it to Ka Bure, the production team leader.

Delong was scurrying through the dense forest when suddenly he heard foot-steps ahead.

He looked up and was taken aback…

Gee! The man walking ahead of him was exactly the man with a black blanket covering his head.

Huh? How come I ran into him?

So, Weila and Ema didn't catch up with him?

The encounter sent Delong's heart thumping hard against his rib cage.

It seemed that the man with a black blanket over his head was heading for the Menglang Mountain Village as well.

*He's going to the Menglang Mountain Village, too?*

*Who's he?*

No matter what, I must trail him and then see what I can do.

But he had just followed a few steps when he felt his heart sink deep…

The man with the black blanket walked out of the dense forest and into the garnet glow of the setting sun. Then, it was clear to Delong that he was having a gray blanket over his head instead of a black one.

*Why, did I identify the wrong person?*

Delong came out from behind the tree and was about to call the man when something completely beyond his expectation happened before his eyes; he was so started that he hastily withdrew the arm that he had reached out…

When the man walked with the gray blanket covering his head, the blanket was caught by a thistle plant, which flipped its corner to reveal the other side. And the color on the other side was not gray, but black!

What? A double-sided blanket!

*Wearing it inside out, he's the man with the black blanket, isn't he?*

Delong was tense with anxiety.

Just then, the man with the gray blanket stopped and turned around. He took off the blanket caught on the thistle plant. The moment he turned around, the opening on the top of the blanket revealed a face glowing with oily luster!

*What? Isn't this Zhe Piao, the blacksmith of the Menglang Mountain Village?*

Not only could he strike iron, but Zhe Piao could also beat silver or repurposing old silverware. Therefore, he was respected by all the villagers.

*What's going on here?*

*Is he a poisonous mushroom among the edible ones as Grandpa Enweng told us?*

*Is he the man who climbed up the dragon fruit tree?*

*But I shouldn't wrong an innocent person.*

*What shall I do?*

*But I can't put the questions to him!*

*Well, I'll pretend not to have seen him in the Wild Bee Valley. I'll ask him about what he did there?*

An idea suddenly struck Delong: I may as well overtake him and wait for him at his home.

Zhe Piao was single and lived at the west end of the village in a bamboo house that the villagers nicknamed "a ghost house." It used to be the residence of a witch, who had conducted superstitious practices. After her death, some villagers claimed that they had seen her sitting in the bamboo house burning joss money and drinking rice wine. With the circulation of the claim, no villagers dared to live in it and gave it the nickname of "ghost house." Zhe Piao, however, was not afraid. He slept and struck iron in it.

Delong took a shortcut, passed Zhe Piao, and reached the "ghost house." He peeped into the house through the bamboo fence wall. The "ghost house" was all silence.

He pushed the fence door open, popped his head in, and called out, "Uncle Zhe Piao! Uncle Zhe Piao!"

Of course, there was no answer.

As he walked into the yard, Delong muttered, "So Uncle Zhe Piao isn't home? Well, I really didn't expect it. But how can I come all the way for nothing…?"

He stepped onto the wood staircase, pushed the door squeaking open, and entered the "ghost house."

Zhe Piao never locked his door for the convenience of letting customers in to wait for him.

It was dark inside the house.

Dark red sparks occasionally jumped out the smothered fire pit. A ray of light stole into the house through the rear window. But it was blocked by the thick, and soot-covered wooden column by the fire pit.

Delong pulled over a round rattan stool and sat on it by the fire pit.

He had just taken his seat when, bam, something, which no one knows what, hit the bamboo door.

*Who is it?* Delong panicked. He rose and moved a couple of steps toward the door.

He pricked his ears but heard nothing outside the "ghost house' except the wind.

*It's odd! Who could it be?*

Puzzled, Delong turned around and looked at the "ghost house." It looked ghastly.

Just then, there was a "bam!" on the bamboo door again.

Delong promptly pulled apart the bamboo strips that formed the fence wall and peeped out. He saw a pebble rolling down the staircase but no one in the yard.

*Hey, where did the pebble come from?*

*Is the "ghost house" being haunted?*

Just then, the door squeaked, and a man came in.

At the same time, an arrow flew out of the bamboo grove, through the rear window, and stuck the column in the house.

A small paper roll was fastened to the shaft.

It was a message arrow!

Before Delong had time to pull the arrow out, the bamboo door was suddenly pushed open. Zhe Piao showed up at the entrance, with the blanket folded into a square and carried over his arm. Delong hurriedly rose and shielded the arrow on the column behind him.

"Uncle Zhe Piao!"

"Yes. It's you, Delong. What can I do for you?"

"Yes. I've been waiting for a long time."

"Sorry to have kept you waiting, but I've been to the mountain to deliver sickles."

Zhe Piao's remark caused Delong's heart to skip a beat. Something is fishy here. He's obviously been to the Wild Bee Valley, but how can he claim that he went to the mountain?"

However, Delong did not put his suspicion on his face, "Grandpa's hoe is blunt from use. He'd like you to make him a new one. Could you?"

"Sure I can! When I finish it, I'll deliver it to the apiary!"

"Thank you, uncle!"

"Be seated and have some tea, Delong."

"I…"

Delong could not sit, lest the arrow on the column be revealed.

But refusing to sit would arouse Zhe Piao's suspicion.

As he was caught in a dilemma, Uncle Mowei called out from outside the courtyard:

"Brother Zhe Piao! Brother Zhe Piao!"

Zhe Piao turned around toward where the call came from and responded, "So, it's Brother Mowei. Anything I can do for you?"

Taking advantage of the moment, Delong reached his hand back and yanked the arrow off the column. He then quickly placed it into the deerskin quiver strapped over his shoulder.

He heard Uncle Mowei smiling, "No, Thank you! Lao Liu from the trade company asked me to tell you that the coal you purchased is here. He said you can get it tomorrow."

"Hey, it's really kind of Comrade Lao Liu! I'll go and get it tomorrow." Then he turned around and said to Delong, "Please sit!"

"No, thank you, uncle! I couldn't grope my way back if it were dark."

"He-he-he! Then, I won't keep you here!"

"Bye, uncle!"

Delong pretended to head toward the exit of the village. But he walked around on his way and came to Secretary Lang Shuai's home.

Secretary Lang Shuai was about to go out when Delong came. Surprised and delighted at once, he exclaimed, "Ah, Delong, so you were not eaten by the bear?"

"I'm extremely lucky! Well, Secretary Lang Shuai, how do you know?"

"Grandpa Enweng came to see me with Weila and Ema just now."

Upon hearing that, Delong was very happy, "What? Weila and Ema have been here?"

"Yes, they have. They were trailing the man with the gray blanket and eventually, they caught up with Ka Bure, the veteran production team leader. Ha-ha-ha!"

"Who? They caught up with the Production Team Leader Ka Bure? So the secret about the dragon fruit tree..."

"I was told about it. Now I know everything," Secretary Lang cut Delong short, "But from the way you look, you discovered something new, didn't you?"

Delong removed the deerskin quiver from his shoulder and pulled out the arrow that stood out among the others.

"Take a look at this before I'll tell you everything."

Secretary Lang Shuai took the arrow astounded. He unfastened the small paper roll from the shaft and unfolded it. Two lines of small text were scribbled on the paper:

**The dragon fruit tree has been discovered. Don't cut it down today.**

After reading it, Secretary Lang Shuai held the paper roll tight in his hand and exclaimed "Our enemy is extremely vicious!"

Night covered the border area like the wings of a gigantic hawk.

The mountain wind had just brushed the apiary by the river.

At the moment, the cold blast kerosene lamp still shone in Delong and Weila's shack.

Weila and Ema were lying on their stomachs on the shakedown. They were listening attentively to Delong telling them something.

What was Delong telling them?

About his intense fight with the bear?

No. He had related the dangerous encounter in a breath long before.

About the arrow that hit the column of the "ghost house"?

No! Secretary Lang Shuai reiterated again and again that he was not supposed to tell anyone about the mysterious and vicious arrow. Not only the arrow, but the discovery of Zhe Piao's identity was not to be divulged.

What was Delong telling them anyway?

He was telling them a story that he was not supposed to tell either:

But he could not help. He found it hard to keep it to himself only.

"…tonight, the PLA uncles will catch the villain under the dragon fruit tree and pull the black blanket off his head," Delong was so excited that he held his hands out like an eagle's claws aiming at a bunch of chicks. "Then, we'll know who the villain is!"

"Really?" Ema widened her eyes in disbelief.

"I say, Long-nosed Horse, so we have to wait here like this?"

Weila sat up abruptly.

In fact, he had been feeling anxious. They had chased and chased but ended up running into Production Team Leader Ka Bure. Could he be the villain? What was going on? Now, he was told that the PLA uncles were going to capture the villain, he could not keep calm. He was eager to know his identity.

Delong asked, "Big-headed Horse, what do you think we can do then?"

"I suggest we joining in the battle under the dragon fruit tree immediately."

"Yes, we should pull off the black blanket in person and see who in the world this bad guy is," Ema said with excitement.

Delong said, "Good, we're on the same page. So, it's a deal. Let's go!"

Ema asked, "Shall we tell Grandpa Enweng?"

Weila said, "If we told him, could we go?"

Delong nodded, "Right, we'll apologize to him after we're done!"

The three children thus stole out of the apiary, left Grandpa Enweng behind, and threw themselves into the old-growth forest...

The dragon fruit tree stood silently in the moonlight.

The three children who had sneaked up close were very excited.

"Hey, look! The big tree hasn't broken from the crotch. We're in time to catch the villain," Weila whispered in Delong's ear.

Ema also whispered, "Well, why can't we see any PLA uncles lying in wait?"

Weila responded in a subdued tone, "If you can see them, it wouldn't be an ambush!"

Delong stopped them promptly, "Be quiet!"

After a while, Weila could not keep quiet again, "We're too far off here, so we can't see them clearly."

Delong said, "Okay, let's move a bit closer."

Delong was about to stand up when suddenly a big hand pressed him down on his shoulder. Then a hushed voice demanded sternly, "Don't move!"

The three children were dumbfounded.

Looking back, they found it to be Company Commander Mu Sade!

"Who told you to be here, eh?"

Delong responded, "It's me who took them here."

"Listen, I'll deal with you later. From now on, you're not supposed to move. Don't say anything. Don't even cough…"

Weila asked, "Can we breathe, commander?"

"Of course you can breathe. But you must be quiet. Do you understand?"

At the wave of Mu Sade's hand, "Line-inspector Xiao" crawled over.

"Listen, whatever you do, you must obey Uncle Xiao's orders."

Delong asked hastily, "Ada, what task are you going to assign us?"

"Take cover and wait for orders." As soon as he finished, Mu Sade turned and disappeared in the darkness as stealthily as he had shown up.

"…what orders?" Delong mumbled quietly. He did not quite get it.

"Line-inspector Xiao" ordered, "Listen to me. No one is going to say anything anymore!"

Everyone clammed up and fixed their eyes on the dragon fruit tree motionlessly.

No one knows how much time had elapsed before a phantom-like figure covered with a black blanket suddenly appeared under the dragon fruit tree.

He was seen raising his machete. Swish! He cut off the "silver-backed" vine.

Gosh, the "silver-backed" vine was severed. But nothing happened to the dragon fruit tree.

The tree that should have fallen stood firmly.

Of course, the telephone lines under the tree were also intact.

The man covered with the black blanket was taken aback by this unexpected sight.

Clank! The machete fell to the ground.

Mu Sade quickly jumped behind the man. Before he could dig his gun into the man's back, the man suddenly lifted the blanket and tossed it up to cover Mu Sade.

Mu Sade dodged it. At the same time, he sent the man to the ground on his face with a ground sweeping kick. Not giving up the fight, the man attempted to grab the machete he had dropped on the ground. But unexpectedly, no matter how he tried, he could not move it, as if it were rooted in the ground.

It turned out that Mu Sade had anticipated the man's move and pressed one foot firmly on the machete. Now he added another on the back of his neck. The man struggled hard to move but in vain.

At the same time, thee armed militiamen rushed out from the thickets and leveled their rifles at the man. When the children followed "Line-inspector Xiao" to the spot, the old villain had been trussed up tightly. He crouched halfway down, his wide-open eyes ablaze with a murderous gleam, the nostrils of his fleshy nose flaring with fury, and his big-opening mouth panting heavily.

*Aah! It's Zhe Piao" isn't it?*

It was right. This was none other than Zhe Piao!

Mu Sade said, "You didn't expect this, right? We've reinforced the crotch of the tree. Tell us who made you do this?"

Casting a glare at Mu Sade, Zhe Piao said, "I know nothing!"

Taking a look at his watch, Mu Sade said, "You know nothing? Well, let me tell you something. In three minutes, the bandits that are going to surprise our sentry posts will be greeted by our troops. Of course, the bomb-delivery man whom they are covering won't be able to get away, either. Your task is to cut off our communication so that we would be caught unprepared.

Upon hearing this, Zhe Piao closed his eyes.

Mu Sade ordered, "'Line-Inspector Xiao', Wei Xinong, and you three," he gave the children a nod and continued, "You escort Zhe Piao to the village!"

As he finished, he gave two other militiamen a wave and led them to the border.

Wei Xinong, a militia of strong build, gave the crouching Zhe Piao a kick and demanded, "Go!"

Zhe Piao looked around, stood up, and left with them.

"Line-inspector Xiao" and Wei Xinong escorted Zhe Piao from left and right.

The three children followed Zhe Piao closely.

Zhe Piao was walking with them when he suddenly crouched down.

Pointing at Zhe Piao's head with his gun, "Line-inspector Xiao" questioned, "What are you up to?"

Zhe Piao tilted his head up and fixed his eyes on the water gourd on Wei Xinong's waist. "I want to drink some water."

Glaring at him, Wei Xinong said, "I do have water, but I won't give you."

He had just finished when Zhe Piao bumped his head into his lower abdomen.

Wei Xinong was thrown to the ground with an "Ouch!"

Zhe Piao turned and ran. But "Line-inspector Xiao" held him by the collar. In the jostling, a large piece of his shirt on the back was torn off.

Delong reached his leg and tripped Zhe Piao, who fell on his face. Before he picked himself up, "Line-inspector Xiao" put his gun against his back, "If you run again, I'll shoot to kill you. Get up!"

The lot went on their way to the village noisily.

When they reached the entrance of the village, they ran into the Production Team Leader Ka Bure, who locked Zhe Piao in a granary.

The border remained silent without gunfire until dawn.

The bandits did not make a surprise attack against the sentry posts. Neither the bomb deliverer crossed the border supposedly under its cover.

Mu Sade and Secretary Lang Shuai rushed back to the Menglang Mountain Village, shaking off the dewdrops on their clothes on their way. When they tried to bring Zhe Piao in for question, they found him quite dead though he looked as if he were fast asleep.

"I'm not a coroner. I'm here to pull some answers from his mouth!"

Mu Sade raked his eyes over the faces of the people watching over Zhe Piao:

The veteran Production Team Leader Ka Bure, Wei Xinong, and the three children.

A black cobra suddenly slithered out from Zhe Piao's crotch, issuing from its throat a terrifying sound:

Hiss! Hiss! Hiss!

# Chapter 5

The moon rose and fell; the stars faded and returned.

The PLA troops waiting in ambush with an intent to wipe out the bandits crossing the border had been lying there for four days and four nights. But nothing abnormal had happened.

The old banyan tree by the valley river were in light yellow buds. More than a dozen colonies of bees had been added to the apiary of the Menglang Mountain Village. These new bees had lived in grottoes, tree holes, and earth caves. With a tenacious character and diligent work ethic, they had gone through trials and tribulations inflicted upon them by nature. But they had lived an unyielding life from generation to generation. It was Delong, Weila, and Ema who had led them out of the old-growth forest to the sunny apiary, enjoying their new life in cozy beehives.

The children took especially good care of these bees. They would collect large-size banana leaves at night when moss floated to the surface of the valley river from its bottom and when the wind came whistling from the old-growth forest into the apiary bringing with it the bellows and bleats of muntjacks and red deer. With the banana leaves, they pleated into pieces of attire and put them over the beehives to keep the sleeping bees warm. During the day, when the sun scorched the banana leaves like bonfires and heated the air so much that even cicadas stopped chirping, they would go to the valley river to carry fresh water back to the apiary and sprinkle it over the hives and the grassy ground around them so that cool and humid breeze could be blown into the hives. They would prepare the bees special mess for each meal, such as more nectar and salt solution so that they were well fed.

Under the upmost care of the children, the dozen or so colonies of new bees were very happy. They flew singing their joyous buzzing songs all day long. When stars fell as dewdrops and twinkled among the thick growth of grass, they flew out of their hives in throngs to look for flowers and collect nectar. When the moon rose and sprinkled myriads of silver nuggets into the valley river and veiled the old-growth forest with white silk, they turned the nectar that they had collected during the day into honey. Some bees regurgitated the nectar from their bellies while others sucked it into their bellies and regurgitated it again. The bees repeated the process for about a hundred times before they could produce drops of amber-colored honey. The dozen or so colonies of new bees had produced quite a lot of honey in a matter of a few days.

This afternoon, two or three screams of owls were heard coming from the old-growth forest. Grandpa Enweng said that when owls hooted during the day, rain would be imminent. Sure enough, before long, a curtain of mist began to unfurl and hang from the sky. The bees in the apiary all hunkered down in their hives. None of them dared to venture out because a single drop of rain dripped on their wings would deprive them of their ability to fly.

However, the drizzle was no big deal to the children.

After finishing their homework assigned by their teachers, Weila took Delong to the valley to collect mushrooms. Ema remained to help Grandpa Enweng harvest honey from the honeycomb that they had cut in the morning.

Harvesting honey is an interesting job. Each small piece of a honeycomb is crowded with numerous cells sealed with covers of beeswax, and each cell is filled with honey. Getting honey from the cells is called honey harvesting. Grandpa Enweng's bamboo house was home to a honey-harvesting machine made of bamboo strips and a wooden barrel. It was very easy to operate. It just required honeycombs being fed into the bamboo baskets in the wooden barrel that that was to be turned with a cranking bar. Once the wooden barrel was turned, sweet and aromatic honey would ooze out of the small bamboo tube attached to the bottom of the wooden barrel.

At dusk, Delong and Weila returned with a good harvest of mushrooms.

Upon entering the apiary, they saw Grandpa Enweng feeding nectar to the bees alone, carrying a log skep in his hand. *Well, where's Ema?* Grandpa Enweng replied, "Mhm, after she helped me harvest honey, she's gone to the valley river to angle. She said, when you guys are back, we'll cook a pot of fish and mushrooms and enjoy a scrumptious supper."

"Wow, Ema's getting more courageous now, no longer afraid of a bear pinching her ear anymore." As he said so, Delong offered to take the barrel from Grandpa Enweng, saying, "Grandpa Enweng, you can take a break. I'll feed the bees."

Weila said, "Let me do it!"

With that, he grabbed the wooden barrel, but in doing so made it swing. Consequently, some of the honey was spilled onto a beehive. Grandpa Enweng hastily wiped if off.

Weila asked, "Grandpa Enweng, why are you wiping it? The bees will soon lick it up."

Grandpa Enweng said, "Hey, you're wrong! We must wipe it up, otherwise, there would be a war. The worse scenario would be a war entered by all the bees in our apiary."

Scratching his head, Weila asked in doubt, "What? What do they start a war for?"

"That's because you challenged them to war!" Grandpa Enweng beamed, "This is called 'bee robbery.' When you sprinkled some honey on the beehive, bees from other hives would come to rob the honey. Then the bees of this hive will fight the bees from other hives. Then all the bees in our apiary would come and take part in the battle. Some of them would be allied with the bees of one party and others with the other party. Then such a tangled warfare would result in heavy casualties and cost our apiary dearly!"

Sticking out his tongue, Weila said apologetically, "Oh, my, we'll be more careful when we feed bees in the future."

Delong might have had a good supper, but he could not have a good sleep. For several nights, when he closed his eyes, he would see the ghastly "ghost house." He would then hear a swoosh and found a bamboo arrow with a secret letter attached to it running into the house's wood column. *Who shot the bamboo arrow? How could he have learned about the secret of the dragon fruit tree so quickly? Who told him? Zhe Piao must have known this person. But it was just at this critical moment that he was bitten to death by a cobra. When did the cobra sneak into Zhapiao's crotch? Did it sneak into it of itself, or someone placed it there? Then who was it? At the time, apart from the three of us, there were also the Production Team Leader Ka Bure and the militiaman Wei Xinong in the granary. Could it be the Production Team Leader Ka Bure? Covered in the black blanket, was he really collecting the glossy ganoderma...?*

His train of thoughts was as lengthy as the silk from the cocoon. So many questions prevented him from falling to sleep.

Tonight, the frogs croaked especially louder. Ribbit! Ribbit! The ribbits came from the west and the east. It came from this side of the river and the other side. The chorus of the frogs kept Delong wide awake and gave his mind free reign to fly to the apiary.

In a sultry night like this, queen bees and baby bees would find it hard to go to sleep as well. In this case, worker bees from each hive would gather at the entrance, where, facing out, they flapped their wings to fan air into the hive to cool the nests off. But this was also the moment when frogs lying in wait would stick out their tongues to capture and swallow them one by one.

As he thought of this, Delong could no longer lie on the shakedown. *No, I must drive them away!*

Weila felt Delong tossing and turning all the time and asked half awake, "Are you bothered by fleas?

"No, by frogs." Delong rose and grabbed Weila by his ear. As he shook him, he said, "Wake up! Wake up, Big-headed Horse."

Weila felt pain in his ear. Wiping off saliva from the corner of his mouth, he asked, "What are you doing?"

"Did you hear how much the frogs are croaking?"

Weila was now wide-awake, "Oh yes, they're eating our bees now. Let's go! Let's catch them!"

"Let's go!"

"Shall we wake Ema up?"

"Nope! Let her have a good sleep!"

Delong had just finished when a voice came from outside the shack, "Who came up with the wicked idea?"

*Jeez! It's Fairy!*

"I was awakened by the frogs long ago. I'm here to wake you up!" said Ema.

Thus, the three children came to the apiary hand in hand.

Frogs are amphibious, breathing with both their lungs and their skins, which are always slimy. The oxygen in the air is filtered through the skin. The more dampen the environment is, the livelier they become. When the air is arid, they will take shelter in mud holes. In such a cool and refreshing night like this, hopping and jumping gaily, they are especially hard to catch. You may see one sitting in the grass croaking with its sacs puffed into lumps, but when you pounce on it trying to catch it, it will slip through your fingers and vanish into thin air.

The three children worked hard in a frantic rush. After a long while, they were as exhausted as frogs crouching on the ground. Peace and quietude came back to the apiary again.

What to do with the captured frogs?

Of course, they were let go in the valley river as usual.

The nightly wind was cold and gloomy. The stars twinkling in the dark blue sky, some seeming chilly, some warm. The dark, dense forest in the Wild Bee Valley appeared like a giant monster looming before the children. The valley river vaguely visible behind the thickets looked like a python coiling itself around the monster-like dense forest. The mountain wind flapped the tips of the trees of the forest, as if the monster were battling with the python while bristling its hair. The starlight was floating on the river, as if the python was wriggling its body to tighten its grip on the monster.

The three children went into the thicket by the valley river along this familiar path.

They were about to reach the edge of the water when all of a sudden, there came a splash. They stopped stunned. Then another splash followed. Still another.

Delong looked at Weila, who glanced at Ema in turn, but none said anything. Together, they trained their eyes on the source of the splashing sound at the same time.

It was a dozen or so steps away from the children. It seemed that either a fish had flipped onto the sand beach or a water snake swaying its tail as it dived into the river.

Pulling apart the branches of the shrubbery in front of him, Delong popped his head out to observe…

Gee!

The ghastly white starlight lit up the surface of the river, and the thicket on the riverside extended obliquely into the water. Somewhere between the river and the thicket, there squirmed a terrifying long face!

This face was extremely ugly. The snout extended more than half a meter long. When it opened its mouth baring two rows of sharp teeth, it seemed to halve its lumpy face. The dermal scales on its forehead were so thick that its eyes were nowhere to be found. With the writhing of this face, a crocodile slowly appeared from the river.

"When it loses its temper, it could bite our foot off. We'd better not say hello and let it alone," Delong hushed his voice.

Taking refuge behind the bushes, the three children huddle together, holding their breath.

They fixed their wide-open eyes on the old crocodile slowly crawling onto the beach from the valley river and followed it wriggling into a thicket. A crocodile has a hideous appearance and a violent temper. It often hides in a deep hole under the water and suddenly attacks the fish swimming by. Sometimes, it floats motionless on the surface, looking like a piece of dry wood. Careless long-legged little egrets often alight on its back, pecking up the snails hidden in the dermal scales. When this happens, a crocodile will suddenly sink into the water. Before the egret on its back can escape, it has caught it in its mouth and dragged it into the water. If crocodiles cannot find food in the water, they will clamber ashore on its four short, webbed feet to prey on small animals. Sometimes, it lurks in the grass to ambush rabbits; sometimes it lies on the beach and plays dead. It can remain motionless for a few days. When a crow swoops down to peck at it, it will launch a sudden counterattack. When they fly in a rage, crocodiles can often hurt fishermen. Therefore, whoever sees their ferocious-looking faces will inevitably feel scared to various degrees.

Normally, when the old crocodile dragged itself along into the distance, the children could come out to let go their frogs. However, no one had expected that when the old crocodile got into the thicket, the pale starlight suddenly revealed a creepy scene:

The old crocodile stood up like a person!

It shook the drops of water off its body, and walked into the old-growth forest on two legs.

What?!

The children were so astonished that they barely cried out.

*How can it be?*

*Who has seen an old crocodile walk erect like a person?*

"A water monster! A water monster! A water…" exclaimed Ema, holding Weila's arm, trembling all over.

"Don't be afraid, Ema! You've got two horses here. We can run away at any moment!" After he tried to calm Ema down, Weila nudged Delong on his waist, "As if we were imagining things!"

Delong said, "It's not an old crocodile. It's a person!"

"A person?" Delong's conclusion scared Weila and Ema.

"Yes, a person in a crocodile's skin!"

"Why did he disguise himself as a crocodile?" asked Ema.

"A good guy wouldn't do this, would he?" Weila wiped the cold sweat off his forehead and responded, "He thought he could fool us!"

"What do you think we should do? Catch him?" Delong asked Weila.

"No, we'll follow him and see what he's up to!"

"Great! You're getting smarter! Let's do this. We two shadow him. Ema, you hurry back to alert Grandpa Enweng. He'll know what to do!"

"No, I won't leave you. I want to be together with you guys…," said Ema.

"There's no time to wrangle over who's to do what. Hurry," said Delong. "It's dark, so open your eyes wider as you walk!"

"Lift your feet higher!" added Weila.

"Okay. You take care, too!" Ema reached her hands out reluctantly.

The three children held their six hands tight together. Then, they parted company decisively.

Ema took the narrow path leading back to the apiary whereas Delong and Weila went into the thick forest in the Wild Bee Valley.

It was dark in the old-growth forest, but they could still see half-distinctly the "old crocodile" tottering in the moonlight leaked through the thick foliage.

Delong and Weila walked cautiously. They followed and followed, not knowing for much distance they had covered. Suddenly, Old Crocodile stopped under a red cedar tree and quickly disappeared.

"Jeez, he's entered the tree hole, hasn't he?" Weila whispered in Delong's ear.

Delong shook his head, "No! Look, he's 'laying eggs' under the tree!"

Standing on his toes, Weila peered at the man cloaked with a crocodile skin. Sure enough, he was burying something under the red cedar tree. After he finished, he went on his way.

Delong and Weila immediately came to the base of the red cedar and located the spot where the earth was loosened. They raked off the top soil with their hands and was surprised to see, in the soil exuding an odor of decomposed leaves, a sealed transparent plastic bag. In it there were three mungo-size iron balls. A small clock was attached to the fuse of each of them.

Weila exclaimed, "Gosh, he did lay some eggs!"

"These terrible things are time bombs!" Delong said in a hushed tone, "I've seen things like them in the armory before."

Delong saw them in the armory indeed! It was after an ambush battle. Delong had come to the armory to see his aha who had been wounded by the arm. Upon entering the armory, Delong found the trophies piled on a board bed, such as rifles, handguns, and hand grenades. Delong knew all the trophies except for two mango-size iron balls. He was about to pick one up when Platoon Leader Yang stopped him and told him that they were time bombs-bombs controlled by a timer. One could tell them to blow up at any time they set.

"Time bombs?" Weila widened his eyes as soon as he heard Delong's introduction. "Now I see. It must be aimed at the armory!"

"We're really lucky!" said Delong as he took the bombs out of the earth pit. "The bandits planned to send them across the border a few days ago but changed their mind. Now, they've delivered them in a different way but unfortunately they've fallen in our hands."

Weila held Delong by the arm and said, "Hurry! Let's go. Let's catch this Old Crocodile before he escapes!"

Delong shook his head, "Old Crocodile is not a grazing lamb. If he broke our legs, then the bombs would fall into his hands again, wouldn't them?"

"Then, what shall we do?"

"How about this, Weila. You go back to the village and take the bombs to Secretary Lang Shuai.

"You shadow Old Crocodile yourself?"

"Yes!"

"No, it's too dangerous for you to do it alone!"

"Don't argue anymore. We must part company at once. We must leave the red cedar tree as soon as we can. Maybe someone will come to retrieve the bombs!"

"What? Someone who'll come to get the bombs?" asked Weila. "Who can that be?"

"Maybe he's hiding in our Menglang Mountain Village, like a little egret flying back and forth in front of us…"

Weila suddenly had an idea. He cut Delong short, "Delong, go after Old Crocodile. I'll remain here and see who's coming to get the bombs!"

"You remain here?"

"Yes, I'll climb up the tree!"

"Hide on the tree to see clearly who'll come to get the bombs?"

"Yes. You may rest assured!" Delong raised his head and took a glance at the luxuriant foliage of the red cedar tree and was certain that it could keep people from being seen. He pulled Weila into his arms and held him tight. "Good for you! Let's do it. Since you've got the bombs, don't get down from the tree even the sky collapses!"

"Don't worry, Delong!"

They thus said goodbye to each other.

Gently patting his bosom where he stowed the three bombs, he quickly climbed up the red cedar tree like a squirrel. Then he hid himself in the dense foliage, through which he watched out for what was going on below. He was up there for no one knows how long. Tired of sitting, he crouched. Tired of crouching, he straddled a bough. With the clouds floating in front it, the moon sometimes faintly shone on the trees and sometimes threw the old-growth forest into complete darkness.

Then, footsteps were heard shuffling beneath the tree.

*Someone's coming!*

Weila quickly pushed aside the leaves in front of him and through the crack saw a dark human figure coming toward the red cedar tree.

Weila was so excited that his eyelids twitched.

However, before he could take another look, a piece of cloud floated in front of the moon. The old-growth forest was plunged into total darkness. Nothing was visible.

*Darn! This piece of cloud came at a moment when I'm just ready to draw my bow. The wretched cloud! The wretched cloud!*

Weila was anxious as an ant on a hot pan.

He leaned down and opened his eyes as wide as he could, but he could see nothing.

In the pitch darkness, Weila heard clearly the footsteps stopping under the red cedar tree. Then he heard the sound of digging. It then stopped before long. The man under the tree sounded as if he were greatly disappointed. And then, the sound of shuffling began to sound under the tree again.

The footsteps went away further and further and eventually died off in the old-growth forest.

Weila was more anxious.

*Am I going to see him slip away through my fingers? No! I won't let that happen!*

Weila could not stay on the tree one more second. He wanted to climb down and chase the man…

Just as Weila was about to climb down the red cedar tree, Delong was trailing Old Crocodile as nimble as a lynx trying to catch a rabbit.

Delong was hot on the trail of Old Crocodile. He walked and walked, past tree after tree, through thicket after thicket. Gradually, Delong came to realize Old Crocodile's intention: He was heading to the valley river in a roundabout way.

Then he would sneak into the river and cross the border. *You want to flee? No way!*

Delong was pussyfooting when all of a sudden he tripped over a vine hidden in a thicket. Thrown out of balance, he was falling. He reached his hand out and grasped a small tree. But the momentum shook the tree so much that it startled something on top of it. Cackle! Cackle! A startled little egret took its flight giving a few eerie cries.

Hearing a startled little egret crying, Old Crocodile suddenly turned around. Meanwhile, Delong stooped down and promptly hid behind a thicket.

The thick foliage blocked Delong's view so that he could only prick up his ears and listen quietly.

Shuffling! Shuffling! Shuffling! Soon, Delong heard footsteps coming from the thick growth of grass in front of him.

The footsteps might be as light as a snake slithering into the grass, but to Delong, each step sounded like a heavy drumstick beating his chest.

Shuffling! Shuffling! Shuffling! The sound of footsteps was closer and closer.

Delong knew that Old Crocodile was closing in.

*What shall I?*

Cold sweat broke out on his face. He fumbled about himself for something but found nothing that he could use as a weapon. He then reached his hand out and ran it over in the grass in a haste. Suddenly, it hit a pebble and hurriedly picked it up. But it was smaller than his fist and had neither edges nor corners. *How can I use such a pebble as a weapon?* Bracing for the onslaught of Old Crocodile, he grappled the pebble so tight that his palm was wet by the sweat it was exuding.

With the approaching of the footfalls, Delong's heart beat faster and faster. Thump, thump, and thump! He swallowed hard lest his heart might jump out of his mouth. He swallowed and swallowed until his throat was dry and burning. *Well, Old Crocodile, bring it on! I'll crack your skull with the pebble. Your time bombs are in our hands anyway.*

Just at the critical moment, the footsteps stopped sounding. Then, Old Crocodile went away shuffling and shuffling. *He didn't see me?* As he thought so, Delong wiped the cold sweat from his face. He gently pushed the bush branches apart and peered into the front.

*Ahh, Old Crocodile is gone!*

Only the back covered with dermal scales undulated in the thicket.

Delong was delighted and felt a great relief, as if a fully drawn bow was relaxed.

He slowly straightened up and was about to resume his pursuit…

When all of a sudden, a gust of ghastly wind sprang up from behind!

Delong turned around. Jeez! With the gust of wind there appeared a ferocious face. Before he could evade it, a pair of plier-like hands had clinched his neck tightly.

Delong suffered suffocation and saw stars. The man

gave him a kick in the back of his right knee, and his leg gave, bringing him collapsing down to the ground. As the two hands let go his neck, Delong opened his mouth trying to gasp for air when a big foot stepped on the back of his neck, pressing his face on the grassy ground. His brain went blank. With his head pinned on the ice-cold earth, he could not move at all.

"You damned daredevil, this is what you've asked for by following me!"

With that, Old Crocodile pulled out a knife from his waist and thrust it downward…

Where was Ema while Weila risked climbing down the red cedar and Delong's life was hanging in the balance?

Right now, Ema was unconscious…

After parting company with Delong and Weila at the riverside, Ema had stumbled back to the apiary like a startled muntjack. She rushed to Grandpa Enweng's bamboo house where the cold blast kerosene lamp was still on.

She had just stepped on the staircase when the door opened squeaking.

Grandpa Enweng reached out his big hands and pulled Ema into his bosom, "Fairy, you're running so fast. What has happened?"

Ema could no longer hold her tears. While gasping for air, she told Grandpa Enweng everything, "A water monster…oh no, an old crocodile…"

"Really? Don't be scared, Ema. You have your grandpa here. No matter how fierce a wild animal is, it won't scare a mountain hunter like me." While calming Ema down, he began to dress and arm himself: He put on his headwear, slung his long machete over his shoulder, placed his crossbow and quiver on his back, and grabbed a blunderbuss in his hand. When he was ready, he crouched down, held Ema's shoulders around his arm, and said, "Ema, listen! Your grandpa is an old tree. You, Delong, and Weila are three young boughs. Now, grandpa is going to look for Delong and Weila…"

"I'm going, too. I'm going with you!" Ema cut her grandpa short.

"No, you can't. Grandpa will give you an important assignment." As he said so, Grandpa Enweng took down the kerosene lamp hung on the house's wooden column and continued, "Ema, this kerosene lamp is my eyes. I will see you accomplish your task."

"Grandpa, what do you expect me to do?"

"Go to the village and see Secretary Lang Shuai. Tell him that I've gone to rescue the children and ask him to look for us with his people. Good girl, time is hard pressed. Do what I'm telling you. Let's set out together!" As he said so, Grandpa Enweng walked out of the bamboo house, taking Ema by her hand.

A gust of wind assailed them and nearly blew off the flicking lamp.

Grandpa Enweng hastily took out a box of matches and said, "With matches, you don't have to worry about your lamp being blown off. Hurry, get this and hit the road, my good child!"

Holding grandpa's hand, Ema surveyed his loving face and the greyed hair sticking out of the headwear in the lamplight. "Grandpa…"

Patting Ema on her shoulder, Grandpa Enweng said with a smile, "My child, don't worry about me. Your grandpa's eyes are given by a leopard; ears by a muntjack; waist and limbs by a tiger; and strength by an elephant. I'm afraid of nothing!"

The grandpa and granddaughter thus said goodbye to each other and each went their own way.

Grandpa Enweng's figure vanished in the darkness of the night, and the kerosene lamp shone on the winding path leading to the Menglang Mountain Village.

To pass the information on to Secretary Lang Shuai as soon as possible, Ema did not take the main road. Instead, she followed a short cut, a narrow, meandering footpath which led to a precipitous hillside. The kerosene lamp looked like a firefly that flew and flew. Startled snakes slid away by her feet. Nocturnal bats on patrol skimmed across the top of her head. A big, fat porcupine blocked her way with all its quills erect.

But none of these could stop Ema's progress. She knew clearly how important each of her step was.

Just as she could see the village, thump! she was tripped over a rock! She, along with the kerosene lamp, rolled off the hillside.

Her head bumped into a tree, and after seeing stars briefly, she became senseless…

A burst of cold, gloomy wind blew out of the depth of the remote valley and rustled the grass on the slope.

In the swaying grass, a pair of green eyes glowed, fixed on the motionless, unconscious Ema.

These are the eyes of a leopard…

# Chapter 6

The wind laden with nightly dew caressed Ema's forehead like a cool hand. The sweat-soaked, freezing cold clothes, clung to her body. The unconscious Ema shuddered and opened her eyes.

*Why? Why am I lying here? Where're Delong and Weila? Where's Grandpa Enweng?*

Ema looked at the starry sky and then the thick grass covered with dewdrops. She quickly remembered everything: *My task is to pass important information to Secretary Lang Shuai. Everyone is waiting for me!*

The thought gave her strength. Ema pushed herself up and stood on her feet.

Suddenly, a gust of chilling wind assailed her, and it was imbued with a strong fishy odor.

Ema looked up, only to see a leopard approaching threateningly.

The leopard had meant to steal into the village to capture a piglet. But the accidental tumble of Ema down the hill with her kerosene lamp scared it into the thick growth of grass. There, it observed her closely and found her not only nonthreatening but also big enough to stave off its hunger pangs.

While swallowing its saliva, it prowled toward Ema tentatively. It closed its left eye and kept the other open for a while, and then vice versa, so that its eyes were like two dim, green lights, flashing intermittently in the grass.

Having nowhere to run or hide, Ema was so distressed that she could not even cry.

Suddenly, a whiff of kerosene drifted over in the wind. It brought Ema's eyes to the source, the broken kerosene lamp, from which kerosene was leaking. Wow, kerosene! Fire!

Ema recollected herself and became confident: Fire can frighten the most ferocious animal in the world.

She remembered the box of matches that Grandpa Enweng had given her. She felt for it, and found it still in her pocket. *Now, I've got my life saver!*

Ema produced the matches, lit one with a strike, and "boosh!" the grass soaked with the kerosene started burning.

The sudden flare of the flames terrified the leopard. With a roar, it turned and took flight, its tail rustling the bush branches all the way behind. After it scampered for a quarter of a kilometer, it paused and stole an unresigned glance at the fire burning increasing fiercely.

Ema unscrewed the round fuel-tank cap and poured the remaining kerosene on the fire. Boosh! The flames jumped higher.

Panicked, the leopard took to its heels.

"The leopard is scared away! The leopard is scared away!"

Ema cried out with joy. Wiping the sweat off her face, she gathered the dried-up branches and twigs on the hill-side and threw them into the fire so that it burned more brilliantly. The brisk flames painted the crags red, the ashes soared into the midair and began to descend, the long tongues of fire wagged up and down.

"Oh, fire. Burn! Burn!" The flames excited Ema, who cried out loud, "Please burn more briskly! Even more! So that Secretary Lang Shuai can see you. So that the villagers can see you!"

Tonight, none of the occupants of a bamboo house in the Menglang Mountain Village was asleep.

A long iron chain hung from the soot-blackened eaves to somewhere above the middle of the fire pit. An oblate pot was hanging from the chain. The tongues of the flames from the fire pit kept licking the bottom of the pot. The water in it gurgled and tried to escape from under the lid in the form of steam.

Taking the pot down from the hook of the chain, Secretary Lang Shuai refilled Company Commander Mu Sade's enamel mug. The big tea leaves in it immediately gave off a whiff of intoxicating aroma.

"…Our opponent is extremely cunning!" Secretary Lang Shuai refilled the tea and continued, "We've just caught Zhe Piao, and they killed him with a cobra."

"Yes," Mu Sade nodded, "He's prepared for the worst. On the one hand, he had told Zhe Piao not to cut down the dragon fruit tree. On the other, he had the cobra ready. When we intercepted the poisonous arrow and caught Zhe Piao, he quickly got rid of him. Obviously, our opponent is among us. He knew we had set up the ambush under the telephone pole No.109. He knew that the secret about the dragon fruit tree was disclosed by the children. He knew that Zhe Piao was captured alive. And he knew that we laid an encirclement like an escape-proof net. He told everything to the bandits across the border so that they changed their action plans."

Brrring, brrring, ringaling! The telephone on the bamboo table rang urgently and interrupted Mu Sade.

Mu Sade picked up the telephone. It was from Platoon Leader Yang from a sentry post…

Patrols found that someone had crossed the border through the shallow part of the valley river. While crawling on the riverbed like a crocodile, he grabbed the pebbles and rubbed the moss on them, thus leaving his trace behind. The sentry post had dispatched two detachments to search for him along the river.

Mu Sade told Platoon Leader Yang, "I'll be there immediately. When you look for the target, you must spread out and take cover. Do you understand?"

"Yes, I do," responded Platoon Leader Yang.

Mu Sade hung up and was ready to set out.

Secretary Lang Shuai stood up by the side of the fire pit, "They're coming again!"

Company Commander Mu Sade responded understandingly, "Yes, they're coming again. They find it impossible to come by land, so now they're trying to cross over from the water."

Just then, the sound of footsteps was heard from the wooden staircase. "Line-inspector Xiao" shouted at the top of his lungs, "Fire! Fire!'

Both Mu Sade and Secretary Lang Shuai were stunned.

What "Line-inspector Xiao" referred to was exactly the fire set by Ema.

When the firelight called Company Commander Mu Sade to her, Ema was so excited and she did not know what to say. After a long while, she threw herself into the arms of Company Commander Mu Sade, tears rolling down in torrents.

"Delong, Weila, and also grandpa…they all went to the Wild Bee Valley to catch the bad guy, an old bad guy in a crocodile skin…"

Secretary Lang Shuai rose abruptly, "The two children are in grave danger!"

Company Commander Mu Sade looked up: The Wild Bee Valley was veiled in total darkness…

…In the dark, dense forest, Old Crocodile had pulled a

knife from his waist. He was thrusting it downward...

Delong struggled desperately, shaking his head, winking his eyes, puffing his cheeks, and gurgled in his throat. He tried all he could to indicate that he wanted to say something.

But, without showing any hint of hesitation, Old Crocodile pushed the knife down.

Before driving it into Delong's chest, Old Crocodile abruptly flicked his wrist. Squelch! The knife was planted in the muddy ground.

"Well, you have something to tell me?" Old Crocodile laughed malignantly, "I wanted to ask you, too. Listen, if your cry out, I'll twist your head off!" As he said so, Old Crocodile held Delong by his hair and twisted his head aside, and the knife planted erect in the mud left a cut on his neck, from which blood oozed slowly. "Did you hear me, eh?"

Delong felt so much pain that he twitched his mouth.

Old Crocodile dragged Delong's head up by the hair and demanded, "Spill it!"

Delong stuck his tongue out and licked his chapped lips, "If you killed me, you wouldn't be alive even if go back!"

"What? What did you say?"

"I said if you killed me, you would be going back alive!"

"Nonsense!"

"I'm not talking nonsense!"

"Why?"

"I've dug out your time bombs!"

"What?" Old Crocodile's color came and went as he grappled Delong by his collar, "What did you say?"

Unlike Old Crocodile, Delong felt relieved, "I said we had dug out the time bombs, three in total, right?"

"You're courting death!" cursed Old Crocodile in anxiety, "Where did you put the bombs?"

Delong clammed up.

"Damn it! Where did you put my bombs?"

Delong said, "Even if I told you, you wouldn't believe me."

"Tell me!"

"I hid them somewhere."

"I don't believe you," Old Crocodile said as he gave Delong a shove. "Go, take me to where you hid them."

In the moonlight, Delong spotted another crocodile wavering in the thicket. Oh, it turned out that this guy had taken off his crocodile skin and hung it on a tree. *Well, let's wait and see!*

Digging the tip of the knife in Delong's back, Old Crocodile threatened, "Hurry! If you're pulling my leg, I'll kill you with a single stab!"

Delong did not budge. He had originally planned to run away when he had promised Old Crocodile to take him to the bombs. But he had not expected that Old Crocodile would have wanted to go to the red cedar tree. *That would be terrible because Weila is still on the tree watching for someone to retrieve the bombs. In case the person hasn't come while Delong is still on the tree, it would be too dangerous: Weila will certainly come down to my rescue when he sees me coming! If that should happen, we both would suffer and end up losing both our lives and the bombs. Delong could not think further. He prayed silently: Weila, oh, Weila, please be calm. Never ever come down for my sake…!*

While Delong was uneasily pondering, Weila was seeing him in his mind's eye.

Sin the moon was blocked by cloud, Weila did not see clearly who had come to retrieve the bombs.

He thought very hard as what to do. Eventually, he decided to get down from the tree to go after the mysterious person.

Suddenly, his shirt was caught by a branch. As he was untangling it, he touched the bombs in his bosom, and Delong's voice began to ring in his ears: You've got the bombs. Don't get down from the tree even if the sky collapses!" This was the warning that Delong had given him before his departure!

For a time, Delong seemed to stand solemnly in front of his mind's eye, looking at him sternly.

Weila felt his ears burning with shame. And his limbs froze. Holding the tree, he was at a loss. After a long time, he climbed back into the foliage. *Okay, I may just hide here until Ema brings people over. Anyway, the person to retrieve the bombs has come and left empty-handed, and I've been waiting for nothing. If I should get down and risk encountering something unexpected, then it would be more than waiting for nothing!*

After thinking hard, he decided not to climb down. He would wait no matter what. He was confident that Ema would be able to bring people here.

But, before long, a new challenge presented itself to him.

Shuffling! Shuffling! There came the sound of footsteps under the red cedar tree.

Weila listened carefully and identified the footfalls of two people.

*Is Ema coming with Grandpa Enweng?*

Pulling the foliage apart gently, Weila was dumbfounded!

It gave him such a shudder that he nearly fell from the tree.

It was Delong who was walking up to the red cedar tree. His hair was shriveled and his clothes tattered. Tagging after him closely was a man holding a knife in his hand.

Rage flew through Weila like lava! He felt his eyes burning, his heart thumping, and his head about to pop!

*Delong is a captive of the old villain!*

*No, I must get down from the tree! I must get down to his rescue!*

His hands trembling, Weila could not stay put anymore.

*But how to rescue Delong?*

*Climbing down? Then any stir on the tree would alert the old villain. No, that won't do.*

*Dropping the bombs to hit the old villain wouldn't work either. If I missed him, the bombs would be returned to him. If they blew up, not only would the old villain be killed, but Delong would also become the victim of collateral damage!*

I'll just find the right opportunity to jump from the tree on to the body of this old villain to pound him to the ground on his face!

*Then I'll stamp his head with the "hoof" of this Big-headed Horse, and he would be half dead for sure.*

*Yes, this is a perfect plan.*

Having made up his mind, Weila clenched his teeth and tightened his waistband. He fixed his eyes on the old villain, ready to have a go. He was looking for the right moment to do it.

Just then, Old Crocodile took Delong to the red cedar tree. Grabbing him abruptly, he ordered, "Stay put for me!" Then, he crouched down to dig up the loose mud under the tree.

This was a good chance for Weila. He swallowed repeatedly and shifted, trying to aim his body at that of the old villain.

While Old Crocodile concentrated on digging for the bombs, Delong raised his head stealthily to search for Weila while he prayed secretly: *Weila, please don't come down. Don't do it! Never even attempt it!*

Suddenly, he saw Weila and found him getting ready to jump.

Oh, no! Don't do it!

Delong's eyes were burning with anxiety: *Weila, don't jump! If Old Crocodile dodged, you would crash and severely injure yourself! Please don't jump. Just leave me alone. Don't worry about me. Your task is to keep the bombs safe. Do you understand? Do you?*

For a while, Delong had a lot to say to Weila, but he could not. He was so anxious that sweat broke out all over him.

*Delong, don't worry! I'm coming. I'm coming quickly to your rescue! Weila also murmured silently on the tree. I'll jump and ram the old villain to death. Voila! We'll claim our victory…*

Weila was making up his mind to jump from the tree when an arrow on a crossbow stuck out from behind a big tree in the vicinity of the red cedar. The poisoned arrow was aimed at Delong…

At this moment, Delong had concluded that Weila would definitely jump from the tree to help him and he could do nothing to stop him. While he was at a loss, he suddenly hit upon an idea in desperation: He turned around and ran!

The arrow was launched at the same time…

"Ouch…"

A heart-wrenching cry of agony.

But it was Old Crocodile, not Delong, that collapsed.

When Delong had turned to run, Old Crocodile had sprung up to go after him, and in doing so, he had become the fall guy.

The arrow had been dipped in rank poison. That was why Old Crocodile gave only a single cry and fell motionless.

Unaware of Old Crocodile's death, Delong ran like mad!

Seeing Old Crocodile fell dead with just a scream, Weila was also scared and was at a loss what to do.

*Who did it?*

Hiding on the tree, he searched with his eyes but saw no one coming over. He listened hard but heard nothing, either.

Weila sensed that the archer had no good intentions.

*A good guy wouldn't have done this!*

Weila hid on the tree for a while and found everything quiet below.

*The villain is dead, but Delong doesn't know it yet. Where did he go? I must tell him not to run anymore and that we can go back to the village together.*

But what about the bombs?

I may just as well fasten them to the tree and come back to retrieve them.

Weila took out the plastic bag containing the time bombs and hang them over a crotch. He tore a piece from his shirt and fixed the bag with it. Then, he slid carefully down.

Down from the red cedar tree, Weila groped his way in pitch darkness through the old-growth forest. He was groping and groping when suddenly he felt a gust of ghastly wind sneaking up from behind. Before he could look back, a big hand had gripped him by his shoulder.

Weila broke out in a cold sweat. He turned around only to see a wizened face in the ghastly moonlight.

Argh, it's Ka Bure, the production team leader!

He had a machete on his waist, a crossbow and arrows on his back, and a blunderbuss in his hand. He was in a perfect outfit of a hunter.

Weila was stunned at first and then became delighted, "Production Team Leader Ka Bure, hurry! Let's go and find Delong! We ran into the old villain…"

Upon hearing this, the Production Team Leader Ka

Bure shuddered a bit, which Weila could feel from the hand on his shoulder. Ka Bure then said, "Muntjacks of the same brood stay together in life or death. But why did you leave Delong alone?"

"I…" Weila meant to tell him everything in a breath but suddenly, the image of Ka Bure covered in a black blanket at the Wild Bee Valley flashed before his mind's eye. His heart jumped a beat, and he swallowed what he was going to say from the tip of his tongue. He said to himself quietly: *Weila, Weila! Don't tell anyone where the bombs are hidden!"*

The otherwise straightforward Weila, now said after a few seconds of thinking,

"Old Team Leader Ka Bure, this is what happened: after we discovered the old villain, Delong asked me to report him. But the forest is so big that I milled around…"

Before he finished, a gunshot came from the old-growth forest…

Bang!

Production Team Leader Ka Bure and Weila were taken aback…

Now, Delong was running like a wind. He ran and ran until he felt there was no one trailing.

*Hey, Old Crocodile isn't catching up!*

*I'm free?*

Delong slowed down. Then, he stopped to take a breath.

Suddenly, a man came out of the forest.

Delong was shocked, "Who is it?"

"Me!" the man answered as he walked up.

A fixed look assured Delong that the man was none other than militiaman Wei Xinong.

He carried a blunderbuss in his hand, a machete on his waist, and a crossbow and a quiver of arrows on his back.

Delong immediately recognized him, "Brother Wei Xinong! Brother Wei Xinong!"

"Yes!" Wei Xinong put his arms around Delong and responded.

"Brother Wei Xinong, how come you are here?"

"My blunderbuss was bored of staying at home, so I came to the old forest along with it. Why are you here?"

Delong was so delighted that he spilled everything.

Wei Xinong kept nodding his head as he listened, "You guys are great, Delong! Hurry up! Let's go to find Weila at the red cedar tree. It's too dangerous for him to keep the bombs alone!"

Delong agreed, "Yes, in case he gets down the tree and runs into Old Crocodile, he would be in serious trouble!"

Wei Xinong said, "You're right. That's what I'm worried about!"

Delong led Wei Xinong to the red cedar tree.

From a distance, he spotted the tree and cried out joyously, "Brother Wei Xinong! Look, that's it!"

As soon as Delong turned around and reaching out his hand to point at the red cedar, Wei Xinong drew his dagger, aimed it at his back, and swung it downward…

# Chapter 7

"Who're there? Are you Wei Xinong and Delong?"

Wei Xinong had just drawn out his dagger and was about to push it into Delong's back when someone called out loud from the forest.

Wei Xinong recognized Grandpa Enweng's voice and broke out in a cold sweat. He flicked his wrist and withdrew the dagger into his sleeve and quickly put the same hand on Delong's shoulder. "Delong, listen, it's Grandpa Enweng!"

Hearing Grandpa Enweng's voice, Delong responded in all excitement, "Grandpa Enweng, it's me! It's me!"

"Delong! Delong! De—long!" Grandpa Enweng shouted, and he was so excited that he even struck a wrong tune. He staggered over like a toddler and pulled Delong in his arms. "My child, my good child! My little red deer…"

As Grandpa Enweng said so, beads of tears rolled down his cheeks one after another from the quivered corner of his eyes and dripped onto the face of Delong. "I've been looking for you here and there. Ema told me everything. I knew you ran across an 'old leopard.' While I was looking for you, I dared not to call you out loud for fear that I might startle the leopards. So, it was so hard to look for you. I was so anxious that I felt my heart almost broken…"

Delong felt a twinge in his nose and started shedding tears. He had so much to say but was unable to say anything. What he did was hold Grandpa Enweng tight and call him repeatedly, "Grandpa Enweng! Grandpa Enweng…"

Grandpa Enweng wiped the tears off his face and ran his quivering hand over Delong's head, "Aww, aww, grandpa is here. Grandpa is here. Everything's okay. I've finally found you. Well, Weila? Where's Weila?"

"He's…still on the red cedar tree! He wanted to make sure which villain was going to dig out the bombs!"

"I see! Great! Great!" complimented Grandpa Enweng.

Only then did Delong realize that Ema was not with Grandpa Enweng. "Grandpa Enweng, where's Ema?"

"She's coming! She's coming! Everyone's coming! The people she was supposed to summon are all coming! Didn't you hear a flock of hawks are coming from the old-growth forest?" Grandpa Enweng's words were imbued with joy.

Wei Xinong was stunned, "Well, I didn't hear anything!"

"For a hunter, you ought to hear it unless your ears are plugged with muntjac's droppings!"

As he had jeered, Grandpa Enweng had straightened his back, raised his blunderbuss to aim at the sky, and pulled the trigger...

Bang!

This was the gunshot that the Production Team Leader Ka Bure and Weila heard.

With the gunshot, the sound of numerous footsteps was heard coming from the forest. As it happened in a fairytale, a large number of people suddenly appeared from under the ground and crowded over from all directions.

Grandpa Enweng shouted at the top of his voice, "Hey... there! Hey...there! Our little hero Delong is here!"

Delong jumped in excitement and held Grandpa Enweng in his arms, "Grandpa Enweng, why did so many people come from?"

"Haven't you figured out? Patting Delong on his shoulder, Grandpa Enweng grinned from ear to ear. "Among these people, there're PLA soldiers, village militiamen, Secretary Lang Shuai, and Production Team Leader Ka Bure. There're also Ema and Weila. There's probably your ada, too!

They've all had a hard time looking for you! Call back! Call back! Hurry and call back!"

"Alright! I'll call back. I'll call." Standing on his toes, Delong called at the top of his lungs, "Hey…there! Hey…there! I'm here!"

Wei Xinong also joined in the excitement, "Come over here! Come over!"

"Hurray! Hurray!" The old-growth forest was filled with the cheers. The people who had scattering around in search of Delong all heard his call. Here and there appeared innumerous flaming torches that suddenly illuminated the old forest.

At this moment, Delong's sentiment was beyond words.

"Delong! Delong!"

This was from Weila. He rushed over with the Production Team Leader Ka Bure.

The two young friends held each other tight and then rolled on the ground…

# Chapter 8

It was a beautiful morning. While dewdrops were still sleeping on the blades of grass, the bees began to buzz around. Like beans rolling, they vied with one another in existing the entrance of each hive. They flew to the woods in threes and fives and began their busy day of work.

While the bees were bustling, the three children set to work as well. A few colonies in the apiary required separation, but they did not have enough hives. They had to find hollowed trunks in the old-growth forest to make log skeps. They went with a small spade, which they would use to dig some wild yams and editable herbs.

Along their way, their talking point centered around Old Crocodile, whose death of a poisonous arrow was dubious. Who shot him? Who was the one that came to retrieve the bombs? That night, Weila ran into Ka Bure whereas Delong bumped into Wei Xinong. They were both armed with bows and arrows. Could one of them be the killer...

A lively conversation went on with everyone joining in. They came up with more questions than answers. As they chattered, they entered the Wild Bee Valley without realizing it.

The tall tropical almond tree was like a huge green umbrella blocking the sky and the sun. It was a perfect place for them to cool off. The island lychee trees extended their huge radiating buttress roots trying to impede their advance...

But nothing could stop them from moving forward.

The three children kept walking.

A peacock ascended from a Ficus hookeriana Corner tree, spreading its colorful tail to flaunt its beauty before their eyes. A skylark sang melodiously to perform for their ears. A red deer, wavering its antlers to tantalize their young curiosity. A Tibetan sand fox, holding a dried-up twig in its mouth, jumped splashing into the valley river. When all the lice in its hair escaped to the twig to avoid being washed away by the water, the fox tossed the lice-laden twig far away and clambered ashore. Then it shook the water off its body so that the little droplets spread as if they were flowers sprinkled by the fairies from the sky...

However, nothing could catch the children's attention. They looked and looked, concentrating on looking for hollowed tree trunks.

Suddenly, there came a strange sound from the thickets nearby:

Bleat, bleat, bleat!

Bleat, bleat, bleat!

Delong said, "It's the cry of a female muntjack!"

Ema added quickly, "It's coming to water by the river!"

From Weila's expression, it followed that neither Delong nor Ema was correct. He shook his big head and said with a drawl, "Nah...nah! Muntjacks don't cry in broad daylight. It's the deer call used by a hunter."

"A muntjack call?" Ema widened her eyes. "Why is a hunter calling muntjacks with a female muntjack call?"

"He must be using it to lure muntjack bucks!" said Weila. "I heard ada said that hunters blew muntjack calls to mimic the cry of a female muntjack, and muntjack bucks would come out the thickets..."

Before Weila finished, Delong cut in, "Look! It's Wei Xinong who's calling muntjacks with the call!"

Weila and Ema stood on their toes and peered into the direction that Delong was pointing. They saw Wei Xinong carrying a blunderbuss in one hand and a black muntjack call in the other. His shadow flashed and disappeared. Then, the bleats of the muntjack call drifted out of the dense foliage again.

Bleat, bleat, bleat!

Bleat, bleat, bleat!

Suddenly, a big, brownish hairy head popped out of the thickets.

Ema cried out, "A muntjack buck! A muntjack buck!"

"Don't yell! This is not a muntjack buck! It's a wild buffalo. It's tough to deal with. Let's run!" said Weila as he took flight pulling Ema by her hand.

Delong also sensed danger and ran desperately with them.

They ran not because they were chickened out, but because they knew that wild buffalos were really ferocious, and even leopards were scared of them.

The three children galloped for quite a while. When they found the wild buffalo not on their trail, they stopped. Pressing their hands on their chests, they gasped for air.

Weila peered into the distance for a few seconds and suddenly yelled, "Jeez! That's not a wild buffalo. Come on and look! It's got a big copper bell!"

Delong and Ema took a closer look. Sure enough, it was a big yellow ox. As soon as it came out of the forest, it started grazing, as if oblivious of what was going on around it. A big copper bell was hanging below its neck.

Ema wiped the sweat off her forehead and heaved a sigh of relief, "Phew, it was so scary!"

Delong said, "This ox is not from our Menglang Mountain Village. Ours have bell of the round shape, but his one has an oblong bell."

Weila said, "You're right! Where does it come from?"

Delong responded, "Let's go and take a look!"

The three children went toward the yellow ox.

Docile as it was, the yellow ox was focusing on grazing. Glistening in the sun, the brown copper bell was pretty lengthy, as long as a bamboo tube. It shone in a tarnished brownish luster. The bell was engraved with a beautiful pattern of lotus flowers. Due to weathering, the grains of the pattern were covered with bluish green verdigris.

This was an ox raised by an Aini farmer.

Delong suddenly said, "Weila, listen!"

Weila was startled, "Listen to what?"

"The ox bell!"

"The ox bell?" Weila was perplexed, "What's wrong with the bell?"

But soon, he was really confounded...

As the yellow ox was moving, the bell swayed to and fro but gave no sound at all.

Ema also cried out, "The big copper bell is mute!"

*What's going on?*

*Is the bell broken?*

"Let's capture the ox and find out. Domesticated cows don't gore people," said

Delong with a wave of his arm.

However, before the children approached, the ox mooed, erected its tail, and aimed its horns at them, with its head tipped to one side.

Stretching its neck, Delong fixed its eyes on the yellow ox. Suddenly, his eyes sparkled. He abruptly threw himself to the ground and raised his head. When he looked into the bell, he exclaimed, "Gee! The bell was stuffed with a clump of grass!"

Crammed with grass, the bell was certainly mute.

*It's strange! Why is the bell filled with a clump of grass?*

The children's interest was instantly aroused.

Just then, the bleat of the muntjack call came from the forest again.

Bleat, bleat, bleat!

Hearing the sound, the yellow ox already assuming a fighting posture waved its ears.

Bleat, bleat, bleat!

The muntjack call kept sounding from the forest.

Suddenly, a sharp noise produced by something unknown came amid the bleating sound.

Whistling...whistling...

Upon hearing it, the big yellow ox gave a loud "moo" and galloped into the forest like mad.

The silent bell swayed to and fro under the ox's neck.

"Let's chase it!" Delong emphasized his order with a wave of his arm. Shouting "Charge," the children sprang up and went after the ox running wild.

The ox soon disappeared in the forest.

But it left a trail of hoof prints behind on the muddy ground. The curious children traced them for a while and suddenly heard mooing in the dense forest ahead of them.

Ha! The big yellow ox was just in the front!

The children were reinvigorated.

Sharp-eyed Ema spotted the ox first, "It's there! It's there! The big yellow ox is too tired to run. It's too tired to run!"

Delong and Weila looked in the direction that Ema was pointing. Sure enough, the yellow ox was really too exhausted to move further. It stood still panting.

The children ran a few more steps, and then it became clear that the big yellow ox was not unable to run anymore. It could not move because its horns were taken hold of by someone. This person held its horn in one hand and fumbled about in the bell. He was trying to dig something out.

"Brother Wei Xinong!" shouted the children as they hurried up to him.

There was no mistake that the person who grasped the ox by its horn was none other than Wei Xinong.

"Hey, there's something in the bell. You see, the ox's bell was stuffed with a clump of grass!" said Wei Xinong as he withdrew from the bell his hand holding the grass. "I blew my muntjack call to attract muntjacks, but I never expected I would run into this creature. I also found its bell mute and was puzzled." As he said so, Wei Xinong gave the big bell a push, and it sent forth resonant ding-dong, ding-dong, and ding-dong!

Though the ox bell was not mute anymore, the three children felt a bit disappointed somehow.

Wei Xinong said, "It's apparent that this ox is released into the wild by some farmer from the other side of the border.

"Ox released into the wild?"

"Yes, you may not know. The farmers on the other side of the border are different from us. We either pen our cattle or herd them by professional cowherds. But they just set their cattle free in the wild when they don't use them. Their cattle then eat and sleep any way they want. When the time comes to using them, they'll find them in the old-growth forest. This is called releasing cattle in the wild. This particular one must have been crossed over by itself. It happened a lot before. So, let's set it free."

Scratching his head, Delong asked, "The old-growth forest is very deep. Once let free into it, how can the farmers retrieve them when they're in need?"

"Well, they trace the sound of their bells. Each of them has an ox bell!"

Delong blinked his eyes, thinking: *It's weird! If they trace the sound of the bells to their cattle, then why did they plug this ox's bell up with a clump of grass?*

Just then, there came someone from the thickets. It seemed to be Production Team Leader Ka Bure.

Ema called out, "Team Leader Ka Bure! Team Leader Ka Bure!"

She called several times, but Team Leader Ka Bure seemed not have heard her. His figure flashed and vanished.

*Well! It was obviously the production team leader, but why didn't he respond? Is it because he didn't hear us or we saw the wrong person?*

While the three children's attention was diverted by the dubious figure, Wei Xinong pulled out his waist knife stealthily and gave the ox a thrust on its butt. The ox gave a moo of pain and ran into the old-growth forest like mad.

Wei Xinong screamed, "Keep away! The ox has shied!"

The children dodged in a haste. In the blink of an eye, the ox vanished in the thick forest…

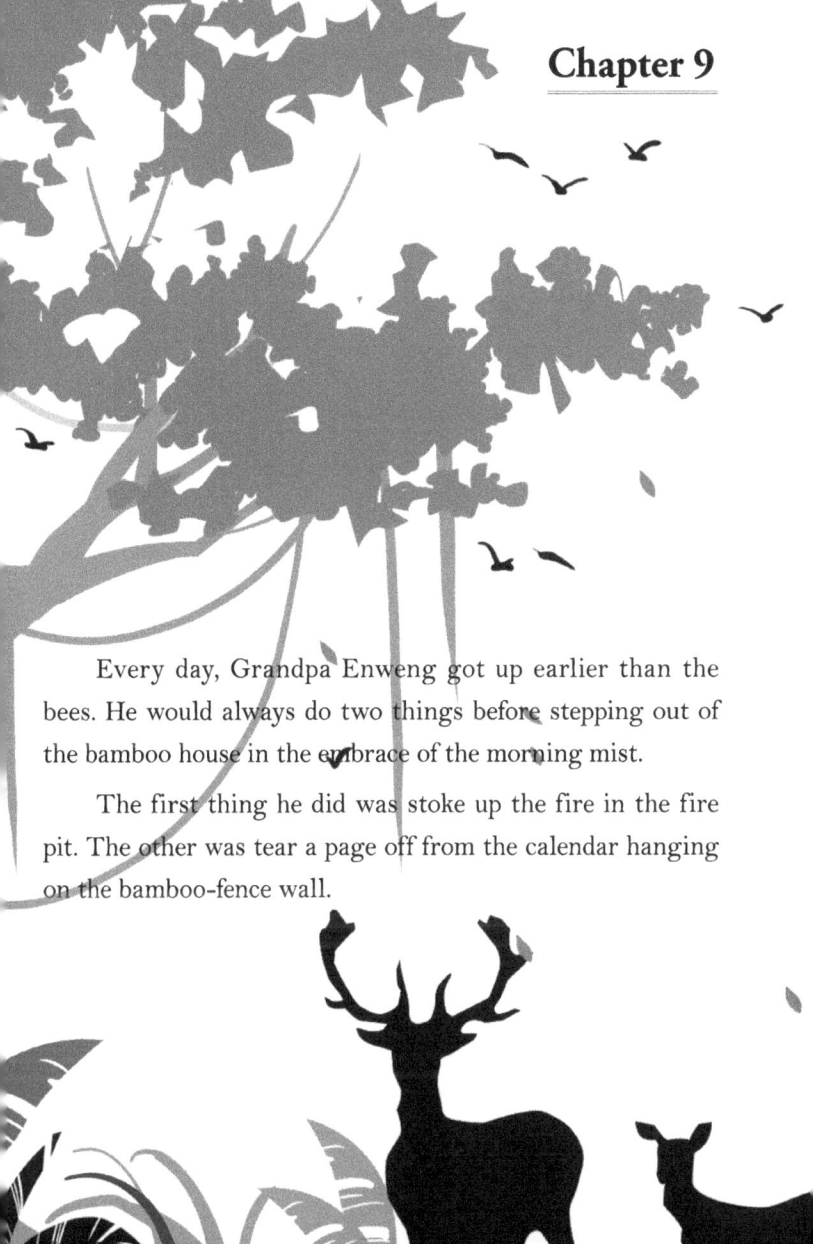

## Chapter 9

Every day, Grandpa Enweng got up earlier than the bees. He would always do two things before stepping out of the bamboo house in the embrace of the morning mist.

The first thing he did was stoke up the fire in the fire pit. The other was tear a page off from the calendar hanging on the bamboo-fence wall.

Every time he tore off a page from the calendar, he would mumble, "Well, a growing bamboo shoot sheds another sheath."

This morning, after he stoked the fire, he was about to tear off a page from the calendar when he suddenly remembered that the children had torn today's page off at noon yesterday. They were looking forward to the Army Day on August 1 in all earnest.

*That's okay. Since it was torn off already, I don't have to do it today.*

It was July 31 today.

Through the bamboo-fence wall, Grandpa Enweng saw the children getting out of their shacks. Stroking his beard, he murmured to himself, "I see, the day for the peacocks to spread their tails will come tomorrow!"

He then trained his eyes on the twenty big bamboo stems still exuding the fresh scent of the plant. He and the children had cut and brought them back from the valley. They were going to use them to contain the best honey that they were going to donate to the PLA soldiers at the 179th Armory.

Thinking of visiting the PLA tomorrow, Grandpa Enweng could not help humming a tune:

Till twenty strings are broken we've been playing,

Twenty drum heads are punctured by our beating.

Such an excitement in our hearts what is arousing?

The Aini people in the old forest are on air walking.

Though fallen from fatigue my limbs are still dancing.

Even though I'm drunk, I'm still drinking and singing.

Hey, listen, the sound of our singing is undulating,

Look, toasted here and there our wine keeps spilling...

"Grandpa Enweng!"

"Grandpa Enweng!"

Grandpa Enweng's singing was interrupted by the children's calling. Delong, Weila, and Ema rushed up to the bamboo house like three singing and fluttering birds.

"He-he! My sweethearts! Were you startled from your pleasant dreams by the pheasants' crowing or your shacks were dampened by the morning dew? Why are your eyes burn bright than the rising sun and your steps are busier than the bees' wings?"

Grandpa Enweng opened the bamboo door, wearing a loving smile on his broad face.

Delong threw himself at him, holding his right hand in his, "Grandpa Enweng, it's not the pheasants that woke us up. Your song tugged our heartstrings like the wind caressing the branches of the trees."

Weila plunged himself toward him, taking his left hand in his, "Grandpa, it's not the dew that stirred us up with its chill. Your laughter is like the waves made by fish, and we just pricked our ears over the surface of the river."

Ema sprang at him and put her arms around his waist, "Grandpa, what's the date tomorrow? What shall we do today? We couldn't sleep. And you got up even earlier than we!"

"Ha-ha-ha," Grandpa Enweng burst into a guffaw. "Your words are sweeter than honey, and your hearts are gentler than the petals of the flowers. Come, come in!" After inviting the children into his bamboo house, he said pointing at the big honey barrel against the wall, "Look, in the past two weeks, even the bees have read our mind. They have produced more honey than usual, enough to fill twenty long bamboo tubes!"

The children were overjoyed upon hearing it.

Weila said, "Grandpa Enweng, let's fill the tubes with honey right now!"

"Yes, your grandpa knows you're all itching to do this." As he said so, Grandpa Enweng took three bamboo ladles from the bamboo-fence wall and handed one to each of the children. He continued, "You three fill the honey here, and I'll go and inspect the apiary. Filling honey is a cinch; you don't need me to teach you. But remember one thing, it's not like getting water from the river. A bee has to regurgitate and suck nectar about a hundred times to produce a drop of honey. So, never waste it." Then, Grandpa Enweng lifted the lid of the honey barrel. Like the Aini people's legendary fairy Lami Lashan who opened the iron casket of glistening jewelry, he let out a whiff of sweet aroma of honey from the barrel.

"Wow, it smells so delicious, so sweet!" Weila sniffed as his mouth began to water. But he said, "To my mind, we must remember one more thing. That is, when we fill the tubes with honey, we must be careful not to let our saliva drop into them."

Ema laughed, "Go and get two horse feed bags. You and Delong each can wear one over your mouths."

Delong said, "Since I have a long nose bridge, I need a large size." As he said so, he looked into the barrel, only to see it filled with honey, as shiny as resin. "Grandpa Enweng, it's such a big barrelful of honey. It's so much that people can't eat it all in a short time. So, can it go bad?"

At Delong's question, Weila and Ema turned their eyes toward Grandpa Enweng and asked at once, "Can honey go bad?"

"You little red deer! Your questions are more than the seeds in a jackfruit berry! I was just thinking of telling you. There're little bugs hiding in honey. According to the honey purchasing center, they're called 'yeast,' which has a temper similar to that of the mushrooms in the old-growth forest. When it's muggy or rainy, the mushrooms will grow wild from the earth. The yeast can grow wild, too. It's known as fermenting. When they are crowded in honey, the honey will ferment and bubble, rising like dried-up bamboo shoots being soaked through. Then, it will be as sour as unripe grapes." Suddenly, Grandpa Enweng detected that gloom began to spread over the children's faces. He broke into laughter, "Look how worried you guys are! So much so that you've suddenly grown as old as I am! The yeast bugs can run wild, but we know how to suppress them."

Ema asked hastily, "How?"

Grandpa Enweng picked up a bamboo tube and took a piece of white wax from a bamboo basket, "Look! This is what we can do: stopping up the bamboo tube with a cork and seal the rim of the opening in contact with the cork to prevent the yeast from breathing the air seeping into the tubes. Then the yeast will stay calm without fermenting. So long as it remains this way, the honey can be store as long as we like it!"

"That's great!" chorused the children with joy.

Grandpa Enweng added, "Honey has life. It will expand when it's hot. When fill it into the bamboo tubes, we must leave a space as big as our fist from the opening. Otherwise, the bamboo tubes would pop when the temperature gets too high."

The children nodded their understanding and set about working.

They placed a bamboo tube against the honey barrel and gingerly ladled some of the honey from the barrel and slowly filled it into the tube, without wasting a little droplet. When the honey rises a fist away from the opening in the tube, they corked it and placed it against the fence wall. Grandpa Enweng was really good at measuring things with his eyes! The honey in the barrel was enough to fill up exactly twenty bamboo tubes.

When the tubes were all filled and corked, Grandpa Enweng came back from the apiary.

Seeing the twenty filled bamboo tubes, he gave the children a thumbs-up, "Wow. You did a great job! The next step is to seal them with white wax. I checked a moment ago and found we don't have enough white wax. It happens to be a country fair day today. I'll go and buy some wax. Who'd like to go with me?"

All the three children enthusiastically volunteered.

Ema, of course, shouted in the highest pitch, "I'll go! I'll go! Weila broke my mirror. I've long been thinking of buying a new one!"

Weila also cried out, "I'll go, too! I'll go, too!"

"Ha-ha! You're like butterflies swarming a flower. Mind you, don't stamp too much or you'd collapse the floor." Grandpa Enweng eyed the children, his face wreathed in smiles. "I can't take all of you. One of you has to stay and take care of the apiary!"

"Okay, I'll stay!" said Delong.

Grandpa Enweng commended, "Good for you! You're a big brother after all!" With that, he lifted the satchel from the house column, filled it with some food and snacks, and stuffed it into the basket woven with Anji golden bamboo and carried on the back. While getting things ready, he gave Delong some advice, "If it gets too hot, go and get some water from the river and sprinkle it over the hives to cool the bees off. Your lunch is set by the fire pit, so help yourself when you're hungry. Coming in and out of the bamboo house, make sure you close the door. Otherwise, bears will carry the honey-filled bamboo tubes away with them!"

Delong responded, "Don't worry, Grandpa Enweng!"

After that, Grandpa Enweng put the Anji golden bamboo basket on his back and took Weila and Ema with him to the mountain path leading to the country fairgrounds. They were like an old Himalayan blue sheep leading two little lambs hopping and jumping jubilantly.

They had just left when someone pushed the bamboo fence door open.

The Production Team Leader Ka Bure stood in front of Delong...

On the way from the Menglang Mountain Village to the country fairgrounds, there crouched an old banyan tree with a huge crown. It looked crouching because its trunk was so thick that a few people extending their arms could not complete the circle and because it was so short that its branches could catch the headwear of a passer-by. Its dark gray boughs extended to all directions supporting a gigantic, luxuriant umbrella. Beneath it, there were rows of roots bulging out of the surface of the ground giving the appearance of rows of benches. The roots, as glossy as mirrors, demonstrated the tree's ancient age and its magnetic appeal to people passing by.

Roads started here and led to all directions, and people from far and wide had to pass through this place.

However, the most bustling moment was the country fair day.

Like fish entering the river from its tributaries and bees coming all the way to their favorite flowers, people who come to the country fair from different villages, ethnic backgrounds, and both sides of the border all stopped to rest a while in the shade of the big banyan tree. They opened their satchels, took out various kinds of food and snacks, and picnicked amid chatting and laughing. Only when they satisfied their hunger, quenched their thirst, and dried their sweat did they rise, straighten their back, and resume their journey to the fairgrounds. Before their departure, each group of the fairgoers cleaned up everything, placing the remaining food and snacks back in their satchels, and hung them on an accessible branch so that they could retrieve them when they passed by the tree on their way back from the country fair. Sometimes, even after dark and all the fairgoers had returned home, a satchel could still be seen hanging from a branch. Most probably, it could be a case where its owner had forgotten it. He might have run across an old friend at the fairgrounds and they elbowed into a restaurant, where he drank himself under the table. But don't worry. When the next country fair day came, the satchel would still be there. No one had laid a finger on it. This is the time-honored convention among the people here: Each takes care of his or her satchel, and no one touches other's even if it's weathered and tattered.

When Grandpa Enweng took Weila and Ema to the old banyan tree, there were already satchels of various colors hanging from its branches. It was quite a spectacle.

Weila and Ema were enjoying the spectacle with awe, when suddenly Ema cried out tugging at Grandpa Enweng's hand, "Grandpa! Grandpa! Look! What's hanging there?"

Looking in the direction that Ema was pointing, Grandpa Enweng spotted a banana leaf package tied up with a vine. He broke into a smile, "Aha! This must be left by a careless person who forgot his basket carried on his back and came out with only his satchel. He had to wrap his leftovers up in a banana leaf and hang the package there and went to the fairgrounds with his satchel." As he was explaining, Grandpa Enweng removed the basket from his back and took out the satchel from it, saying, "Come on, children. You must be so hungry that your stomachs are touching your backs. While those who catch the early morning section of the fair have gone from here like flying wild geese, let's eat something before we catch up with them."

Weila asked, "Grandpa Enweng, are we going to hang our satchel from the old banyan tree, too?"

"That depends on your stomach! If you have such a big appetite that you can eat a horse and wipe out everything I've brought, then we don't have to hang anything here." As he joked, Grandpa Enweng took out what he had in the satchel one by one. Wow, they were quite a lot: a few rice cakes, a large piece of beef jerky, and over a dozen preserved fish. There were also pickled vegetables, dried termite mushrooms, as well as air-dried red chili peppers, which were thin and lengthy and as red as the flower of the flamboyant tree.

Suddenly, a voice came from the mountain path, "Grandpa Enweng, you're taking the kids to the country fair?"

Grandpa Enweng raised his head, only to Wei Xinong coming over carrying his bamboo basket on his back.

Smacking his lips, Weila said, "Wow, you've got good food here. I don't think you can eat it all no matter how you'll try."

Grandpa Enweng responded, "You're going to the fair, eh? Come and have a bite!"

Wei Xinong said, "I'm going to buy some salt. I had had a big breakfast before I came out, so I'm not hungry yet. I'll leave my satchel here and have my lunch when I come back. I've got a bottle of aged rice wine. Then, we'll enjoy it together!"

As he was speaking, he removed his satchel, chose a branch, and hung it over it. Saying goodbye hurriedly to Grandpa Enweng and the children, he went on his way in a haste and soon disappeared behind the hillside.

Sitting around Grandpa Enweng, Weila and Ema began to eat their lunch. They savored the rice cake, the preserved fish, and the mushroom until they glutted their appetite. Only after loosening their waistbands a bit could they straighten up their back and stand on their feet. Grandpa Enweng picked up the leftovers, wrapped them in banana leaves, and placed the package in the satchel.

Weila took the satchel and climbed up the tree like a monkey. Up there, he hung the satchel high.

When the sun rose to the top of the sky, Grandpa Enweng, along with Weila and Ema, squeezed their way into the center of the fairgrounds. They had to squeeze because the crowd was so dense that it was like the corn stalks stacked in the fields into which no snake could slither.

Taking Weila by one hand and Ema by the other, Grandpa Enweng elbowed his way through the crowd here and there on the boisterous fairgrounds. He purchased some white wax, a small mirror, some student workbooks, and two packages of candies. Later, Weila and Ema were attracted by a stall of the Xinhua Book Store, the largest chain bookseller in China. When they squeezed in, they were amazed by so many books. They were instantly captivated by the picture books with covers of various colorful designs. They lifted through one after another of the books and liked all of them. Finally, Weila selected a few picture books of battles while

Ema picked some books of cats and dogs. However, when they turned around to ask Grandpa Enweng for money, they widened their eyes like the startled eyes of cats and dogs on the book covers: Grandpa Enweng had been swept to no one knows where by the torrent of the crowd!

Panicked, Weila and Ema had to put down the books. They called, shouted, looked, and searched.

But in the hubbub of the fairgrounds, all their efforts were to no avail.

Grabbing Ema by her arm, Weila said, "Let's go back to the old banyan tree and wait there!"

*That's right!* A light sparkled in Ema's eyes. *Since it's hard to find grandpa on the crowded fairgrounds, we'd better go back to the banyan tree.*

When they reached the old banyan tree, Grandpa Enweng had been there ahead of them!

Even at a distance, Grandpa Enweng shouted, "Hurry! Hurry! I've been worrying about you. I've got a very important thing for you to do!"

Weila and Ema were petrified.

Shaking Weila by his shoulder, Grandpa Enweng said, "Why are you so stupefied? Go and climb up the tree to get the satchel!"

"Eh!" Weila sprang up and quickly found himself on the tree, where he unfastened the satchel. He jumped down and handed it to Grandpa Enweng, "Grandpa, what's so urgent?"

Holding Grandpa Enweng by the arm, Ema nudged him, "Grandpa, please tell us now!"

Grandpa did not respond but knitted his eyebrows together. He pulled his waist knife out and unfastened the sheath made of two bamboo strips facing each other. He propped the sheath up against a root of the tree and chopped it with the knife as if it were a piece of firewood. Then, he carved a slanting cross on one of the bamboo strips and cleaved it into two halves from where the two lines of the cross intersected, thereby creating a ledger known as *kemu*, literally "carved wood" in Chinese. He inserted one half of the ledger in his waistband and held the other half in his mouth. Then he quickly opened the satchel, took out three chili peppers, tore a piece of black cloth from his shirt, pressed the peppers on bamboo slip as the half of the *kemu*, and tied them together with the cloth strip. In the blink of an eye, Grandpa Enweng finished it all. Handing the bamboo slip with the chili peppers to Weila and Ema, he said hastily, pointing at a narrow path, "Go now, Weila and Ema, go to the military armory along this path and give this to Company Commander Mu Sade."

Weila and Ema gazed at this strange thing with wide-open eyes and asked in chorus, "What's it?"

"Good children, don't ask. Owls won't scream at day time if it doesn't threaten a heavy rain. I can't say anything before I straighten things up. Hurry! Send this to Company Commander Mu Sade. He will understand as soon as he sees it. Run, quickly! It's not far from the armory! I'm going to stay here and watch out…"

Before Grandpa Enweng said anything further, Weila took the bamboo slip over and stowed it in his bosom.

Taking Ema by her hand, he turned to run. After he covered quite a distance in a breath, he turned around and cried out, "Grandpa Enweng, don't worry about us! we'll send the message to the armory!"

"No, I won't! Go and come back soon!" responded Grandpa Enweng in a raised voice.

Half way up the precipitously craggy Muntjack Hill, there was a limestone cave with a relatively small opening. Concealed behind thickets, it was undiscernible from a distance. Inside, however, the cave was deep and spacious. It was a natural storage space of a considerable volume. Weapons, ammunitions, as well as other goods for military purpose, were piled as orderly as honeycombs. A few well-hidden telephone lines ran out of the cave and slithered like snakes up and over a big tree and disappeared in the dense forest.

This was the 179th Armory that inspired horror among the bandits.

By the side of the road leading to the armory, there stood a tall island lychee tree.

At this moment, Company Commander Mu Sade, Secretary Lang Shuai, and Platoon Leader Yang were together in the armory's sentry post. They were studying a battle plan, and their discussion had lasted a long time.

"...The clues that the children have provided us have further substantiated our observations," continued Platoon Leader Yang as he scanned the narrow path through the lookout window of the sentry post, "By using a muntjack call,

Wei Xinong did not mean to lure muntjacks. He was looking for the yellow ox that had crossed the border by way of a designated method of communication. Later, he spurred the ox away with a knife without Delong's notice. This also tells us that he and the ox has a mysterious connection." Platoon Leader Yang frowned as he continued, "It was so strange: When he located the yellow ox, why didn't he find the bombs in the ox bell but only a clump of grass? Is it possible that the enemy across the border is going to deliver the bombs with another method?"

Secretary Lang Shuai said, "If our opponent still trusts Wei Xinong, then our people would be able to see how the bombs were passed into his hands today."

Company Commander Mu Sade chuckled, "It's a pity that Wei Xinong didn't find the bombs in the ox bell. This means that our opponent doesn't trust him at all. That's why he had him lure the yellow ox with a muntjack call. It was a trick for bewildering us. We've got several clues now, and if we synthesize them for analysis, then we can see things as clearly as getting rid of the moss on the river mud." Throwing a glance at Platoon Leader Yang, Company Commander Mu Sade continued, "Of the clues, some are acquired through your surveillance and some from the children's observations at the sites. One of the children's observation includes a different sound in the midst of the muntjack call used by Wei Xinong…"

Company Commander Mu Sade had just begun when he was interrupted by hurried footsteps.

"Weila and Ema are running over!" Platoon Leader

Yang who was facing the lookout window stood up.

Secretary Lang Shuai turned around and leaned out of the lookout window. He waved at the two children running up.

"Secretary Lang Shuai! Platoon Leader Yang!" gasped the two children with excitement, reaching out their arms like two kingfishers flying toward a bamboo forest.

"Company Commander Mu Sade! Company Commander Mu Sade!"

"What's so urgent?" Company Commander Mu Sade strode toward Weila and Ema, reaching out to hold them in his arms.

Weila produced the bamboo slip tied with the chili peppers, "It's for you from Grandpa Enweng!"

Wiping off the sweat blurring her eyes, Ema said, "Grandpa said you'll understand everything when you see it."

"I see. It's a *kemu* with chili peppers," Company Commander Mu Sade held it in his hand, his eyes sparkling, "Where's Grandpa Enweng now?"

Pointing at the path from which he and Ema had come, Weila said, "He's under the old banyan tree with lots of satchels hanging from it!'

By then, Secretary Lang Shuai and Platoon Leader Yang had joined them. Mu Sade exchanged a meaningful glance with them. Then he turned to the two children, "Alright, your mission is accomplished. And you've done a great job! Go and join Uncle Xiao, drink some water and take a good rest. We're going to find Grandpa Enweng and will be back soon."

Holding Company Commander Mu Sade by his big hand, Weila said, "I want to go with you!"

"Me, too!" added Ema.

"Okay! You and Secretary Lang Shuai can come but you guys can take your time." Company Commander Mu Sade then waved at Platoon Leader Yang, "Let's go first!"

Company Commander Mu Sade and Platoon Leader Yang began trotted like two gliding hawks.

Holding Weila in one hand and Ema in the other, Secretary Lang Shuai asked them what had been going on as they walked along.

Like twittering tit chicks that had just hatched, Weila and Ema became two contending chatterboxes. After they finished, Weila asked blinking, "Secretary Lang Shuai, what does the bamboo slip, or *kemu*, mean, the one that Grandpa Enweng asked us to deliver?"

Secretary Lang Shuai explained, "It's a ledger that we call *kemu*, literally meaning 'carved wood,' because the bamboo slip has carvings on it. It's kind of an ancient method of communication used by us Aini people. If the *kemu* has chili peppers attached to it, it means a war was imminent in the past. But now it means that there's something of the utmost emergency to discuss. When one receives this kind of *kemu*, one must rush to the sender. If both parties are strangers, they'll first match the ledger. Only when the carvings are connected into a perfect cross will they begin to discuss grave matters."

I see! After hearing Secretary Lang Shuai's explanation,

Weila and Ema understood everything. It turns out that Grandpa Enweng has something urgent!

Weila shouted, "Secretary Lang Shuai, let's be there on the double!"

"Great!" agreed Secretary Lang Shuai.

The three quickened their pace.

But they were outpaced by what had been happening.

By the time they reached the old banyan tree, Wei Xinong had been captured by Company Commander Mu Sade and his people.

What Grandpa Enweng meant by "utmost emergency" referred to what had happened while he was waiting for the children under the big banyan tree. He had seen a man rammed something in Wei Xinong's satchel and sneaked away. He felt very strange. *Who was this? Why did he break the conventions and messed up with another person's satchel?* He had walked over and was taken aback when he felt the satchel. Just then, Weila and Ema had come, and he had used the *kemu* to call in Company Commander Mu Sade while he had decided to remain under the tree in anticipation for his arrival.

When Wei Xinong had returned to the old banyan tree and started drinking with Grandpa Enweng, Company Commander Mu Sade and Platoon Leader Yang suddenly appeared in front of him. He still pretended not to know what was happening. Platoon Leader Yang rushed over and yanked his satchel from his hands and took out three rice cakes. He broke them off and revealed jet-black time bombs!

# Chapter 10

Night fell. Bees were tired.
The buzz died down in the apiary.

The valley river that had been surging during the day had slowed to a drift, as if gasping tiredly toward the starry sky.

The fire pit was burning brilliantly in Grandpa Enweng's bamboo house.

A pot was set on a tripod. The tongue of flames lipped at its bottom like that of a cow. Grandpa Enweng placed the wax bars bought from the country fair into the iron pot. Before long, the wax melted into sticky and transparent goo. Weila and Ema handed the bamboo tubes filled with honey to Delong. The Delong unplugged each and checked if there was a fist-size space left between the honey and the opening before plugging it and passing it on to Grandpa Enweng.

Beaming with satisfaction, Grandpa Enweng placed the first section of a tube in the melted wax and turned it once. He then handed it back to the children while giving them a kind warning, "The wax is still hot. Mind you, don't scald your hands."

The children were very cautious when they sealed the bamboo tubes and placed them neatly against the bamboo fence wall.

The wax goo on the tubes soon solidified and turned milky white.

The wax-sealed bamboo tubes looked as if they were wearing white silk garments, glistening in the firelight of the fire pit.

While sealing the tubes, they were chatting about Wei Xinong's capture that afternoon.

Grandpa Enweng said, "Children, I often told you that poisonous and edible mushrooms might grow together in the same clump of grass, and bad guys might mingle themselves with good ones. You see, it was totally true. This time, with the capture of Wei Xinong, everything will be clear."

"You're perfectly correct," asserted Weila. "He must have been the one who went to dig up the bombs under the big red cedar tree!"

"He must also have been the one who had shot Old Crocodile to death!" added Delong.

"Children, passing off as a militiaman, Wei Xinong has fooled quite a few people. But a pheasant passing off as a peacock will always find itself short of feathers. Now that he's exposed, everyone feels at ease, and there's no more guesswork." Then, Grandpa Enweng cast a glance at the rear window and continue, "Well, the sky is inky dark. Let's hurry a bit so that we can finish and go to bed earlier. We've got to get up very early tomorrow. The mountain village is closer to the armory so that the villagers do not have to walk a long distance. If we set out late, we'll lag behind."

Grandpa Enweng's reminder spurred the children to work faster.

Before long, they finished sealing the twenty bamboo tubes with wax. Delong worried about accidental leaking. Therefore, he checked the seals around the cork of each of the bamboo tubes. He wanted to make sure that they were all airtight so that no sweet aroma leaked from the tubes. Grandpa Enweng was really an expert in wax sealing. His skill had been honed for many years; for each time he sent honey to the purchase center, he would repeat the same procedure.

After cleaning up everything, they went back to their respective sleeping quarters.

Suddenly, Delong's cry of alarm came from the darkness of the night, "The shack caught fire!"

Grandpa Enweng paled with shock. He rushed out with a bucket of water.

Luckily, the fire had just started. Grandpa Enweng poured his bucket of water and instantly doused it.

"What's the matter?"

Delong said, "My bad! I was too careless and accidentally toppled the small kerosene lamp."

"We're lucky that there's no wind!" Looking at the wet shack, Grandpa Enweng said, "Well, you can't sleep in it."

"Grandpa Enweng, Weila and I had to put up for the night in your bamboo house. We'll rebuild the shack tomorrow."

Weila said, "I've long been wishing to stay in Grandpa Enweng's house!"

Grandpa Enweng said with a smile, "Let's go. Bring your beddings with you."

Delong and Weila thus moved into the bamboo house.

Right at the moment, a tall, lanky shadow covered in a black blanket sneaked under the bamboo house…

It was dawn. The slumbering old-growth forest was awakened by the crows of the pheasants in the valley.

Ema got up instantly from her shakedown and began to dress herself up in front of the newly bought mirror. After she combed her hair, she put on her pretty coned hat. Before she had time to enjoy her looks in the mirror, Weila was calling her at the top of his lungs outside her shack, "Fairy, if you don't fly out of your coop, we'll go first!"

"Hi, I'm coming! I'm coming!"

Getting out of her shack, she saw Weila and Delong already stepping out of the bamboo house, followed by Grandpa Enweng.

"We're going to visit the PLA soon. Let's all load the bamboo tubes!" shouted Delong.

"Yes! Yes!"

The three children vied with one another in placing the bamboo tubes into their baskets carried on the back.

In the blink of an eye, only five of the twenty tubes were left.

Weila was about to load them to his basket when Grandpa Enweng cried out, "Hold! Hold! Leave some to me so I don't have to go empty-handed!"

"Ha-ha-ha!" The children burst into a laughter.

Grandpa Enweng put the five bamboo tubes into his Anji golden bamboo basket and urged the children to set out. They had taken about a dozen steps when he suddenly said, "Geez! While thinking of going early, I forgot to smother the fire in the fire pit. We'd better not let sparks fly again like yesterday!"

Rolling his sleeves up, Delong volunteered himself, "Grandpa Enweng, I'll go and do it!"

Grandpa Enweng said, "The fire that happened to you last night scared the hell out of me. I'd better go myself. I'll catch up after I smother the fire." After he finished, he turned around and headed toward the bamboo house. He did not even remove the basket from his back.

In a short time, he went out of the bamboo house. After locking it up, he caught up with the children and said panting, "It's okay now. I've smothered the fire pit and locked the door. Otherwise, the bears would come and stole all the nectar we've preserved for the bees."

"Grandpa Enweng, do you think the villagers have set off?" asked Delong.

Grandpa Enweng said, all smiles, "Of course they've set out. It's a happy day today for the PLA and the people in the border area. The mountain wind must have pushed open the windows of all the bamboo houses very early!"

Upon hearing it, Weila became anxious. He urged, "Let's hurry up then!"

Just then, a few bees were buzzing joyously away in front of Ema.

Holding her arms up, Ema cried out, "Look! The bees are flying away! What a fine day it is today!"

Swarm after swarm of bees flew buzzing into the distance. The weather broadcast proved to be accurate. On fine days, flowers would bloom better and yield more sweet nectar. The mountain wind could send the fragrance far and wide. Sharp as their sense of smell was, the bees could catch the scent easily. Then they would become uneasy in their hives.

As he was walking, Delong was spellbound by the bees flying by from behind him.

Suddenly, he widened his eyes...

One of the bees flew and flew and eventually winged to the back of Grandpa Enweng. Then it circled around his basket several times and alighted on one of the bamboo tubes. What? The previously smooth wax seal at the opening of the tube had a crack, from which a little honey was leaking. It was this almost invisible smudge of honey that attracted the sensitive bee.

Delong's face suddenly turned ashen white...

It was extremely lively in front of the armory on this festival day. Villagers coming to visit the PLA commanders and soldiers were all dressed in their best.

Just then, a voice screamed booming, "Hey, Grandpa Enweng and the children are coming!" The people turned their eyes to the mountain path. Shouting, cheering, waving, and clapping, they were extending a warm welcome to Grandpa Enweng and the children, who quickened their pace and threw themselves into the embrace of the crowd.

"Sorry, we're late!" His face radiant with joy, Grandpa Enweng held Company Commander Mu Sade by his hands, "The children and I have brought some honey as a token of our appreciation."

Secretary Lang Shuai chimed in, "Company Commander Mu Sade, the children have been looking forward to this Army Day as birds expect the cracking of dawn. I don't have to pester you. You must accept it, discipline or no discipline!"

Company Commander Mu Sade burst into a guffaw, "Secretary Lang Shuai must have borrowed a parrot's tongue today. He's persuaded me to accept all the gifts and left me no alternatives. Okay, I'm now accepting your kind gifts on behalf of all the commanders and soldiers stationed at the armory!"

All the soldiers clapped their hands heartily.

Grandpa Enweng led the children to the cave opening of the armory. Seeing bouquets of fresh flower and various gifts piling up there, he smiled at the children, "Come on, let's place our honey here as well!" As he said so, he removed the basket from his back.

Then, Secretary Lang Shuai and Production Team Leader Ka Bure began to toast the solders. Grandpa Enweng stopped Ka Bure, saying, "Brother Ka Bure, because the PLA soldiers have been working as busily as the bees, we can enjoy our life as sweet as honey. How about serving them the sweetest fine wine to celebrate their holiday?" As he said so, he took out a bamboo tube from his Anji golden bamboo basket. He pulled out the cork, rubbed the opening clear of the wax sealing, and suggested, "Come on, brother, you fill the wine and I'll add the honey!"

"Mix them up! Mix them up!" all the villagers cheered on.

When Secretary Lang Shuai raised his wine cup in front of the PLA soldiers, Production Team Leader Ka Bure and Grandpa Enweng also raised their bamboo tubes and pour the aromatic corn wine and sweet honey into each cup at the same time. The soldiers drank to their hearts' content as the villagers cheered on.

While cheering with the villagers, Delong fixed his eyes on the bamboo tube in Grandpa Enweng's hands…

It was exactly the same bamboo tube that a bee had alighted upon on their way here.

In the midst of the bustling and excitement, Delong told ada his discovery in secret.

Company Commander Mu Sade patted his son on his shoulder beaming but said nothing.

In no time, half of the wine in Production Team Leader Ka Bure's bamboo tube and half of the honey in Grandpa Enweng's bamboo tube had gone.

Grandpa Enweng said to Mu Sade, "Hey, not everyone is here. Where's that Xiao…Xiao…?"

Pointing at the armory, Company Commander Mu Sade responded, "He's working at the telephone exchange in there. Another few soldiers are on guard."

"Well, you're still confining them in the cave on such a celebrative occasion. I do understand that soldiers standing guard can't drink alcohol. But this is not ordinary alcohol. It's a token of festival celebration. If they can't drink a full cup, how about just getting their lips wet? Only then do we think we have fully expressed our appreciation!" While saying so, Grandpa Enweng grabbed Company Commander Mu Sade by the arm and continued, "Let's go. If you don't allow them to come out, we'll deliver the wine and honey to them. We can't leave even one soldier behind! Hey, fellow villagers, tell me if I'm right?"

"Mix them up! Mix them up!"

"Being on guard on a holiday, they deserve more of our appreciation!"

"Deliver the wine and honey to them in there. No one should be left behind!"

The villagers shouted at the same time in response.

"Okay!" Company Commander Mu Sade smiled at the villagers, "We'll let Secretary Lang Shuai, Production Team Leader Ka Bure, and Grandpa Enweng deliver the wine of celebration to the comrades on duty inside so that they can share our happiness!"

After he finished, Company Commander Mu Sade led the Production Team Leader Ka Bure, Grandpa Enweng, and Secretary Lang Shuai into the armory.

But no matter how they wheedled him incessantly, "Line-inspector Xiao" declined their offer adamantly.

"I've accepted your kindness and love, but I'm on duty, and I can't even drink a drop of your wine." Then, he twitched one of his eyebrows naughtily at Company Commander Mu Sade, "Company Commander, this is the discipline you've imposed on us, right?"

Company Commander Mu Sade shrugged, "Yes, I have."

Secretary Lang Shuai said all smiles, "Since it's discipline, we can't lead a horse to the water. But you've got to drink some after your shift, okay?"

"That's right!" echoed Production Team Leader Ka Bure while patting the wine bamboo tube in his hand, "My wine and Grandpa Enweng's honey are offered on behalf of the villagers. Make sure you drink some after your shift!"

"You may rest assured that after my shift, I'll drink to my heart's content. I won't waste the villagers' kindness," said the beaming "Line-inspector Xiao."

Grandpa Enweng said, "I don't think the other comrades on duty will drink our honey wine now. How about this: we'll leave the wine and honey here. Then let them each drink a cup after their shift?" As he said so, he turned to "Line-inspector Xiao" and continued, "We're entrusting them to you, okay?"

"Okay, okay! Leave them to me!" "Line-inspector Xiao" kept nodding.

Thus, Production Team Leader Ka Bure and Grandpa Enweng left their bamboo tubes in the cave.

The two corked bamboo tubes were placed against the bamboo fence wall of the switchboard room.

Behind the bamboo fence wall were the stack after stack of ammunition boxes.

After Company Commander Mu Sade led the people out of the cave, Secretary Lang Shuai hopped onto a big rock and, cupping his hands around his mouth, shouted to the boisterous crowd, "Fellow villagers, please be quiet! Now let me give the floor to Company Commander Mu Sade, alright?"

"Alright!"

Company Commander Mu Sade straightened his uniform to make sure his appearance was in order. He then hopped to the big rock and began to address the villagers in a resonant voice, "Hi everyone, on this celebrative day, you've come to visit us, bringing your deep friendship and precious gifts. Tonight, a grand party will also be held in the village. On behalf of all the commanders and soldiers of the armory, I'm here to express our sincere gratitude!"

A hearty round of applause arose from the crowd.

"Hi everyone! The Aini people have a saying, 'Matches won't ignite until at least there're three.' Before the arrival of the Army Day, you and our company have smashed three attacks launched by the bandits across the border. Our armory stands as firm on this majestic Muntjack Hill as a brave eagle in a storm!"

"Hurray…"

People cheered as loud as the wind sweeping through the forest.

Just then, someone from the crowd yelled, "Company Commander Mu Sade, we saw how you foiled the previous two sabotage plots! What about the third one?"

Company Commander Mu Sade said, "Today, as everyone is here, I'll give you a briefing on the third sabotage attempt."

His words quieted the crowd down.

Suddenly, Company Commander Mu Sade roared, "Lead the ox here!"

With the roar, the sound of an ox bell was bounced from the crag wall of the armory as if it had happened in a fairytale.

People were stunned, but soon they realized that it was the echo of the crag wall.

Their attention was then drawn by a young soldier and a big yellow ox coming out of the forest behind them.

The yellow ox led by its nose ring looked as if had known that it was going to play a major role in a theatrical performance. It walked majestically, the big copper bell dingdonging and ding-donging to the rhythm of its gait.

Company Commander Mu Sade then roared again, "Unleash the ox!'

The young soldier then let go the bridles and, "bam," struck the ox on its rump with a bamboo twig.

The big yellow ox gave a loud moo and scampered into the forest like mad.

"You see? This is exactly the yellow ox that had crossed the border with two bombs in its bell stopped up with grass. Wei Xinong, who had passed for a militiaman, was ordered to get the bombs with the method of calling it with a muntjack call. But when he first used the muntjack call, the ox wouldn't listen to him. It would never listen because it had been trained this way. Let us give it a try. Come on! Call the ox with a muntjack call!"

"Bleat!"

"Bleat!"

"Bleat!"

The young soldier called a few times, but the ox did not respond at all.

Just then, Company Commander Mu Sade took out a bamboo whistle and blew it…

"Whistle! Whistle!"

As soon as the sound of the whistle died away, the yellow ox returned.

"Dear villagers, you've seen clearly today, right? This is how the person who had secretly commanded Wei Xinong with messages attached to his arrows betrayed him. By doing so, he expected us to believe in Wei Xinong's confession and lead us into his trap. What was the truth then? This sinister backstage manipulator, who had sensed that Wei Xinong had been shadowed, devised an elaborate trick: He first called the ox over with a whistle, took the bombs from the bell, rammed a clump of grass in it, and then released the ox. Okay, let us release the ox, too. Come on! Get ready! We're letting the ox go!"

With that, Company Commander Mu Sade slapped the ox on its rump with a bamboo twig.

The big yellow ox took flight mooing into the forest again.

Company Commander Mu Sade continued, "At this moment, Wei Xinong didn't see the ox. He was anxious and used his muntjack call. When it heard it, the ox came back. Now, we'll see how it works. Ready! Sound the muntjack call!"

"Bleat!"

"Bleat!"

The young soldier sounded the muntjack call several times.

Gee, the yellow ox returned indeed.

Everyone was perplexed as to why the big yellow ox returned after hearing the muntjack call. *Didn't he refuse to respond to it a moment ago?*

Company Commander Mu Sade said, "Yes, it didn't respond a moment ago but does now. This shows that it has been well trained. It heard the bamboo whistle first and came, and it heard the muntjack call then and came as well. The yellow ox knows the order clearly. Of course, when it came back to Wei Xinong in response to his muntjack call, the bombs in the bell had already been replaced by a clump of grass. Wei Xinong was made empty-handed. To make us believe that Wei Xinong was the one we were after, the backstage manipulator then played another trick under the big banyan tree with lots of satchels hanging from it on the day of the country fair. He gave up Wei Xinong to us, believing that after we captured him, we would slack our vigilance. Then he can bring the time bombs to the armory in secret today when we're celebrating the Army Day! But he doesn't know that nothing he's been doing has escaped our watchful eyes. Not only has he not escaped our eyes, but he has escaped from neither the eyes of Delong, Weila, and Ema nor the eyes of the veteran Production Team Leader

Ka Bure. The bombs he had hidden in the bamboo tube were deactivated as soon as he left behind him."

"Ah!" exclaimed the alarmed crowd.

"Who's he?"

"Where's he?"

As if to respond to the angry questions,

Thud!

Someone fell to the ground.

He died of self-poisoning, purplish blood oozing from the corner of his mouth...

First written in August 1977 in Kunming
Revised in May 2018